SHIELDBEARER

A MONTAGUE & STRONG DETECTIVE AGENCY NOVEL
BOOK 25

ORLANDO A. SANCHEZ

ABOUT THE STORY

An Aspis never tires. He is the last to fall or falter. He is the shield between life and death.

The Grand Council has designated Simon and Monty as outcasts, deserving of erasure and death. Monty and Simon have vowed to do everything in their power stop the Grand Council.

Power is the issue.

In order to stand against the Grand Council, they must grow in power. In order to grow in power, Simon needs a teacher.

As an outcast, Simon must now perfect his dawnward—the defensive shield he has learned to cast.

There's only one small problem—his outcast status means no one is willing to teach him the advanced version of the cast.

No one, except a mage known as the Spartan.

Now, Monty and Simon will travel to the hidden island of Naxos, where the Spartan is rumored to live. There, they will discover the truth behind the mysterious mage, and what it means to be a true shieldbearer.

Three new worlds. Download three novellas for free.
https://BookHip.com/PZWGAVV

"Come back with your shield—or on it."
-Plutarch

"Imperfection is beauty and madness is genius."
-Marilyn Monroe

DEDICATION

For those who stand in the gap, placing themselves in the breach against all danger to protect those dear to them.

To James Earl Jones
Your voice and presence touched my, and many young lives, and sent our imaginations soaring.

Thank you for filling us with awe and dread.
You will be greatly missed.
RIP
992024

ONE

The sun blazed above the Sri Kailasa temple.

I just wasn't exactly sure it was *my* sun. Peaches rumbled by my side as I took in the impressive stone facade. I looked up at the intricate carvings and marveled at the level of skill required to create the imagery in the stone.

From what I had learned, this entire place was supposed to have been carved from a cliff face. Either I was in the wrong Kailasa temple, or Kali had moved it and I was standing somewhere else.

I had a feeling Jersey was far from where I was standing.

<*Stay close, boy. I don't know exactly where we are, but I don't think this is our plane.*>

<*Where you go, I go. The strong, blue lady smells good.*>

The fact that he could smell her from where we stood only reinforced that he was no regular canine. I glanced over to where she stood. She gave me a look and refocused on the large creature that towered over her.

She looked up into its face without a shadow of fear and said some words I couldn't quite catch, before glancing in my direction again.

<She may smell good—that doesn't mean she's friendly. Stay close. I'll keep you safe.>

<Do you think she will make more meat? I'm starving.>

<You just ate. Don't push it. Unless...you want me to make you some meat?>

<No, your meat breaks my stomach. Ask the blue lady.>

<Later. First, let's find out why she brought us here.>

<To make you stronger.>

<Why isn't it to make you stronger?>

<I am very strong. You need to get stronger. She is here to make you stronger. I am mighty, remember.>

<Of course I remember, you never let me forget.>

<One day you will be mighty too. Don't worry.>

<Not on the top of my agenda. I'm not exactly feeling comfortable about this little visit to her temple.>

<If she attacks, I will stop her.>

I shook my head and smiled at him as I rubbed his head.

<You get full marks for bravery, but we can't take her. She's too strong. Even in our most powerful battleform, she would take us out with barely a thought.>

<This is why you have to get stronger.>

<Of course, I'm the weak link.>

<Frank says admitting the problem is the first step in finding the solution. You can only be dangerous if you are strong. When you are strong, the harmless parts of you are crushed to nothing.>

<That was a very thorough mangling of a familiar quote—you can only be truly dangerous when you are strong, otherwise you are harmless.>

<Why are you repeating what I just said?>

I just shook my head again and scanned the area.

Kali had facilitated our trip to her temple after having a conversation with both Dex and the Morrigan. I noticed I wasn't consulted prior to this trip. Monty stayed at the Montague School of Battlemagic—we really needed to find a shorter name for the place—to practice some new casts Dex was going to teach him.

Secretly, I think he was glad he could pass on this trip; Kali made most people nervous. Being around her was like standing around several thousand pounds of volatile explosive.

One wrong step and it was over.

Having to constantly be in that heightened state of awareness was draining. Granted, I was her Marked One, but I had no illusions as to my safety. If anything, I was in greater danger than the average person.

Her Marked One was held to a higher standard, which was code for one major slip up and I was dust. If she was feeling merciful, she might even bring me back to explain how badly I messed up.

No, I wasn't looking forward to this trip.

Currently, we stood in a U-shaped courtyard of a stone temple complex that was supposed to have been carved out of the side of a mountain. Instead, we stood in the center of three massive slabs of thick, ancient stone, carved with intricate designs and images.

In the center of the three stone walls sat the central temple. Like the mandir I remembered in Jersey, every inch of this stone temple was covered in intricate designs.

Stone obelisks and columns were cut into the surrounding walls; each of them held images of elephants, lions, and turtles. Spread out all over the exterior temple faces, I saw depictions of dancing goddesses.

The dark stone was weathered with age, but held a deep violet glow within the stone itself. There was no way we were in the temple in India. All of these designs were clear and easily seen. None of them were missing parts, which I knew was the case with the temple I remembered.

It may have looked old, but nothing was chipped or

broken. I could sense the energy emanating from the stone all around me. The most impressive part was the size and scope of this work. This temple was easily three times the size of the mandir in Jersey, and every bit as ornate and intricate.

"I thought we were supposed to be in India?" I asked, walking along the edge of the courtyard as Peaches padded next to me. "This doesn't look like India."

Kali turned her head and glanced at me while she created a large sausage for Peaches. He immediately plopped down and began devouring the meat she offered him. Once he reached the end, it rematerialized, forming an entire new sausage.

He chuffed in approval.

<I like the strong blue lady even more now.>

<I had a feeling you would, especially with the infinite meat. Try not to overdo it.>

<How can I overdo it? The meat will never end. This is perfect meat. Can you learn how to make this meat?>

<Not a chance, and I'm not asking either. You would never leave home.>

Kali patted him on the head, which he approved of by nuzzling her hand with his nose, before diving back into the meat devouring.

"He is a good hound," she said, crouching down to rub him between the ears. "He needs to eat more. Are you feeding him adequately?"

I nodded.

"How long will that meat last?" I asked, looking down at my ever-voracious hellhound. "At this rate, he may just explode."

"Until he is sated," she said. "He *is* a hellhound. I doubt he is in danger of exploding."

"Is that safe?" I asked. "You do realize he can eat a substantial amount of meat."

"He will be fine," she said, waving my words away. "What makes you say we are not in India?"

"This entire place is supposed to be carved out from a cliff face," I said, extending an arm toward the temple, "but this is a freestanding temple surrounded by walls. Impressive walls, but not a cliff. Also, I thought this was a temple dedicated to Shiva? Why are *you* here, then?"

"Clarify," she said, as a small smile crossed her lips. "What do you mean?"

"Well," I said, pointing to specific areas, "you have Shiva over there, then he's over there dancing, and then he's over there again, with some woman whispering something into his ear?"

"Parvati warning him about the demon Ravana," she said. "Your point being?"

"And here we stand in front of the central shrine dedicated to Shiva again, and his fairly impressive bull."

"Nandi," she said, running a hand along the stone of the large image of the bull. "Yes, his faithful mount and guardian of this temple. You have yet to make your point, Simon."

"Well, I'm looking around and all I see is a Shivafest everywhere," I said, realizing I was speaking to a goddess of destruction. "Why?"

She glanced at me and shook her head.

"Ignoring the fact that I don't *need* to explain myself, you mean?" she said. "Shiva and I are one. It pleases me to be here. This is Kailasa as it should be, not as it is on your plane, a poor imitation of this majestic and sacred place."

I made a choice to keep my answer to myself.

I was learning.

The fact that she was even answering my questions was surprising to me. Usually, it was all veiled threats and glances of promised pain or death. This time she was actually speaking to me in a conversational tone—not that it fooled me.

This was still Kali the Destroyer.

You didn't earn a title like 'the Destroyer' out of the kindness of your heart. I had no illusions about who I was standing next to. She'd cursed me to what she imagined was a fate worse than death.

The jury was still out on that one.

The last time we met, she was gracious enough to show me what would happen to Peaches and me at the end of his life. It wasn't kind or welcome. The images she shared with me reinforced the one fact I could never lose sight of.

She was not my friend and never would be.

We may have been strolling through an incredible temple dedicated to her lover, but she was still the goddess of death and destruction, with a side of mind-numbing fear sprinkled in for seasoning.

I looked around us and took in the amazing stonework. I had visited the Kailasa in India and been completely blown away by the intricacy of the stonework. This made the temple in India look like a bad copy.

"Why did you bring me here?" I asked. "Couldn't we have had this conversation back at the school?"

"Yes, we *could* have," she said, still looking away. "Then I would have had to explain myself. I don't enjoy explaining myself."

"Never would've guessed."

She stared at me for a few seconds before a small smile played across her lips. She shook her head and kept walking through the courtyard.

Her blue skin glistened in the setting sun. Her jet black hair, which was adorned with gold and ivory accents, was accentuated with a golden disc that sat in the center of her forehead. Her hair danced in the non-existent wind as she moved around the central shrine.

She wore a white, loose-fitting linen top which was edged with softly glowing orange runes, and a pair of dark blue bell-bottom jeans. The bells around her ankles moved with each step, producing a light jingling as her bare feet seemed to glide above the ground.

Even though she looked normal—I mean besides the blue skin, a clear indicator this wasn't Durga, but Kali—I knew she wasn't. I was glad she hadn't opted for the traditional necklace of skulls, or the extra arms, holding an arsenal, complete with a severed head.

No matter how many times we had met, I was never completely at ease around her. Probably had something to do with her cursing me alive and her little moments of torture to teach me life lessons.

Oh, and the Rakshasas.

These weren't the easy-to-gaze-at, animal-headed creatures from some of the stories. No, Kali, being Kali, had to go for the horror deluxe version. Standing around eight feet tall, these creatures were living nightmares, guaranteed to rob you of sleep for at least a week. They had two huge fangs that would make a saber-toothed tiger jealous, and claws that put Wolverine to shame.

Around their necks, they wore a polished silver chain. From the chain hung a glowing violet orb about the size of a grapefruit. Runes covered their bodies, and these too glowed with a faint, violet light.

They stood around the temple grounds at regular intervals, but ignored me and Peaches. I figured since I was here with Kali, I had some sort of immunity.

The last time I encountered them, they were actively trying to shred Monty and me. I shuddered at the thought and had no desire to encounter angry Rakshasa ever again.

"The burden is entirely yours," she said. "Do you understand what it means to be an Aspis?"

"I have an idea."

She raised an eyebrow at me before turning back to admire the central shrine.

"Educate me, if you would be so kind."

It sounded like a request.

It wasn't.

"The Aspis is the name of the shield."

She nodded in response.

"Continue."

"A shieldbearer's role is to protect the vulnerable."

She glanced at me for a few seconds before shaking her head.

"You are no longer a shieldbearer."

"What? You called me an Aspis," I said. "I know I heard you right."

"I know what I said, do you?" she answered. "Why were you made an Aspis?"

"Because cursing me alive wasn't enough torture?" I answered. "Now, I get to protect others while you place my life in constant danger. Like my fan group of successors. Dira is out there leveling up somewhere and getting ready to dust me the first chance she gets."

She sighed and turned to me with a smile that froze me in place.

"Simon, I extend certain liberties to you, because you are my Marked One," she said. "Do not allow my magnanimity to cause you to lose your life...permanently."

She gave me a pointed look which I understood to mean *the ice you are skating on is so thin, you're basically swimming and there are sharks in the water.*

Hungry sharks.

I nodded.

"Got it," I said, becoming serious. "You made me an Aspis, a shield warrior to stand against those who would try to transform and twist the energy I understand as magic into something else, something to hurt others."

"You remember."

"I remember the pain when you did it, and pain is an excellent memory enhancer."

"Indeed," she said. "It is. When you underwent that transformation, I informed you of its purpose. Do you recall?"

I paused for a moment and remembered her words: *You will be my Aspis—my shield warrior. It is not only Tristan that depends on you now.*

"I'm an Aspis, but not just for Monty," I said. "You do realize I can't protect everyone?"

"I am aware. Right now, you can barely protect yourself," she said. "You need help."

"What I need, is to stop the Grand Council."

"How do you propose to do that?"

"I was hoping you could give me a Marked of Kali upgrade," I said. "Something along the lines of a mage eraser ability."

She smiled again and my stomach twisted into knots.

"You cannot face the Grand Council, nor can your mage," she said. "Neither of you are ready. If you do, both of you will die in the attempt."

"That's why I was mentioning the upgrade."

"You don't need an upgrade," she said, glancing at me. "What you *need*, is to unlock the power I placed in you."

"That sounds like pain...again."

She nodded.

"Life is pain, Simon," she said, looking away. "Anyone who tells you differently is selling something. Usually deception. Do you recall the rest of what I told you?"

"Do I have to?"

She gave me a healthy dose of side-eye.

"I could always coax it out of you," she answered. "Is that your preference?"

"No need," I said, quickly raising a hand. "You said I would be tested and that I was the current holder of this title. That there could only be one living Aspis at any one time."

"What does that tell you?"

"That I'm walking around with an enormous target on my back," I said, living dangerously. "Thank you, by the way."

"Actually, it's on your forehead, and it's my mark," she said. "What does being the only living Aspis tell you?"

"Not many people apply for the job because it's high-risk, low reward?"

"Close," she said. "Try again. Think as to why you are here...alone."

"I'm not alone," I said, looking around and not seeing my hellhound. "Peaches—?"

He was gone, and my stomach clenched.

"He is safe, but he will not be able to assist you in this," she said. "Aside from me, right now, you are alone. Why?"

"What about the Raksha—?"

They were gone too.

Normally, this would have made me feel better.

This was not one of those times.

TWO

Kali whirled around and drove a fist into my chest.

I was immediately airborne on a trajectory that led to a collision course with one of the walls that enclosed the temple.

Several things raced through my brain at once as I glanced back.

I could die.

I didn't even see her move, she was that fast.

That wall racing up to greet me looked pretty solid. I was probably going to break something when I hit it.

I could die.

Why would she punch me? She could have waved a hand and sent me flying into the wall. Why take a hands-on approach?

She never wasted energy or effort. It wasn't an accident that she drove a fist into my chest. The heat raging through my body confirmed that my curse was still active. Well, that, and the fact that my torso was still connected to the rest of me was a solid clue that she was limiting herself somehow.

I slammed into the wall back first, and somehow didn't crumple into a sack of broken bones and gore at its base.

"Why are you still alive?" she asked as she headed my way, the embodiment of agony and pain. "That is not a rhetorical question."

"Your curse?" I said, as I slid down the wall and spit up some blood once I reached the ground. "You have some pent-up aggression you need to get out of your system?"

"These quips of yours, do they serve any purpose besides angering your adversaries into inflicting more pain upon you?"

"I...I've found that they really unnerve mages," I managed through a few gasps. "Delicate egos and all that."

"I see," she said, standing several feet away, looking down at me as I slowly got to one knee. "Does it appear to you that I have a delicate ego? That you can goad me into taking an action, any action?"

So many answers available, all of them loaded with the potential for instantaneous and mind-destroying pain.

A tip when facing a god, or goddess in this case: Unless you enjoy massive amounts of pain or have grown tired of breathing, take a pause before answering what seem to be easy questions. Simple and short can save your life in most cases.

"No," I said, getting my breath under control. "It was reflex."

She nodded.

"Your reflexes are decidedly masochistic," she answered. "Why did I strike you?"

Again, it wasn't a rhetorical question. There was a lesson in the midst of all this pain, as was usually the case with her.

"You were giving me a chance to react," I said. "The fact that you didn't just use your power means you're handicapping yourself somehow."

She cocked her head to one side and offered me a raised eyebrow before giving me a nod of approval.

"Beneath all that fear, there is some wisdom," she said. "Why would I handicap myself?"

"Aside from the absolute slaughter it would be if you didn't, since I'm nowhere near your level of power?" I asked. "Honestly, I don't know."

"That's fear speaking," she said, sliding forward and backhanding me across the courtyard. I landed hard and bounced a few times before sliding to a stop across the smooth stones. "Try again."

This was one of those moments when my life choices flashed before my eyes. *Was it still possible to walk away from all of this? Could I alter the path of my life? Did I still have a chance to change everything?*

"No," she said as if reading my mind. "You chose this path, now you must walk it."

"How did you—?"

"Do you think you are the first Marked One to regret his choices?"

"I didn't *choose* to become your Marked One, just like I didn't *choose* to be cursed," I said, glaring at her. "That was all *you*. You did this to me."

I got to my feet again.

This time I was wary, ready for any sudden strike.

She remained across the courtyard, smiling faintly in my direction.

"Feel better?" she asked. "Now that you've placed the blame where you feel it belongs?"

"A little, yes," I said with a nod. "Do you deny it?"

"A valid question," she said. "I'll answer yours, if you answer mine. Do we have a deal?"

That little voice in my head politely reminded me that making deals with divine beings was a losing proposition. I should back away slowly and refuse to answer anything until such time as I could get adequate representation to work out a deal that would work to my benefit.

"Deal," I said, ignoring the voice. "Ask."

"Why do you stay?"

"Huh?" I asked, confused. "What do you mean?"

"It is my understanding that the acoustics of this temple are above par," she said, looking around. "Are you having difficulty hearing me? Did you suffer some recent head trauma?"

She had jokes, but I wasn't going to fall for the bait. Besides, if I answered in kind, I could be taking another unscheduled flight through this temple complex. No, thanks.

"I can hear you just fine," I said as the heat raced through my body, repairing any damage I may have suffered from slamming into the wall and bouncing on the ground. "I just don't understand the question. Stay where? A little context would help."

"Involved, with the mage," she said. "Why do you stay as part of the Montague and Strong Detective Agency? Why not return to the life you had before all of this madness descended upon you? It was certainly quieter. You didn't have to concern yourself with the supernatural, at least not to your overt knowledge. Why do you stay?"

I gave her question thought; it was actually a valid one, a question I had asked myself a few times in the past. I didn't have a good answer.

That was a lie.

I knew why.

"I didn't realize leaving was an actual option," I said. "Where exactly would I go after you cursed me alive?"

She gave me a look that said: *put a little more effort into this*.

"You had options—and still do," she said. "There are many organizations that would pay handsomely for someone with your particular set of skills. Imagine an operator who couldn't die. You could take the most dangerous jobs with no fear of death. You could ask any price, take any risk."

"I walked away from that life for a reason," I said. "Besides, I take plenty of risks these days. Most of them are lethal. It's not like anything has changed in the risk department. If anything they're worse now."

"True, you do have a gift for making deadly enemies," she said. "You still haven't answered my question."

"Purpose," I said. "This life, as screwed as it is, gives me a purpose. Yes, I may be facing monsters every day of the week, mages with delusions of grandeur and ample doses of megalomania, even gods and goddesses, with twisted, hidden agendas, who try to use me like some pawn on a board."

"My agenda is neither twisted nor hidden," she said. "You just haven't learned to see it...yet."

I filed that comment for the future.

"That's why I stay," I said. "This is bigger than me, and I can make a difference. There are people who count on me and I won't abandon them. I protect my home, my city, and if I don't do it while I can, who will?"

"That is quite altruistic of you. Are you certain it's not the excitement, the thrill of facing death repeatedly?" she asked. "I've heard it can be quite addictive."

"Listen, I'm not trying to insult you, but ever since I've met you, I've had enough excitement to last me several lifetimes," I said, shaking my head. "You know what I could get addicted to? Sitting on a beach and drinking my Death Wish without someone or something trying to unalive me. *That* I can get addicted to."

She shook her head.

"That is not your path, you know this."

"I answered your question. Your turn."

"My cursing you was intentional. You say this was all me,

but you are mistaken—this is all you," she said, pointing at me. "*You* were the catalyst for this life you now lead, not me."

"No," I said, risking my existence. "Can you even prove this?"

"You're asking me to prove my words to you?" she asked. "Do you realize how close to the abyss you tread?"

"I would say fairly close, but I'm *your* Marked One; you wouldn't have marked me as yours if I wasn't willing to stare death in the face and keep going," I said, facing her. "So, yes, I want you to prove it."

"Very well," she said. "Remember this request."

The temple disappeared.

THREE

We were standing in my office.

"I need you to apprehend my wife," a voice with a South Asian accent said from the door. I turned and looked at the man. "She needs to be stopped and punished."

I recognized him immediately.

He was tall, dark-skinned, and handsome enough to be a model. His pressed suit flattered him, and I remembered thinking everything about him screamed money.

Shiva.

I looked around and saw the cramped office I used to have. A large desk, some secondhand filing cabinets, and not much else.

I looked to the desk and there I sat.

I glanced at Kali who motioned to past-me with a nod.

"Please let me know if this is inaccurate," she said. "This was your first opportunity to deny my consort, yet you refused."

"It was a job," I said, looking at past-me. "Didn't feel like anything too out of the ordinary."

"Yet you felt the oddness," she said. "You knew something was off even if you couldn't pinpoint it."

She was right.

I had known this client was covered in wrongness; I just hadn't listened to my intuition. Besides, he used the right references.

"He said he was friends with Angel, and he knew about my connection to the NYTF," I said. "He paid well to get me on that case."

"Yes…yes he did," she said, pointing at me. "And you agreed."

I saw myself taking a look at the envelopes Shiva had pushed across the desk in my direction. The stack of hundreds shut up any reservations I had at the time about his name or the strange vibes I was getting from him.

"I did," I said. "That was a mistake."

"The first of many."

She waved a hand and the scene shifted.

We were inside the NYTF, in Ramirez' office.

Monty was hunched over a set of plans.

It was the first day we met.

I still remembered how upset he was at being called a wizard, even to this day. He may have mellowed a bit, but he still didn't appreciate being called one.

He was still cranky as a default mood, just less so. Unless a ruined suit was in the mix, then all bets were off. The scene shifted again and I saw Ramirez sitting in his chair, with Monty glaring at him.

"Sir, I don't think this is an adequate pairing," Monty said as he glared at me. "It's clear he doesn't take this case, or anything, seriously. I've been tracking this around the globe. These people aren't amateurs."

The scene froze at that moment.

"There," Kali said. "You could have chosen to leave. The

mage was right, it wasn't an adequate pairing. You had no idea what you were stepping into."

I nodded.

"I didn't," I said, lowering my voice. "Kids were being taken. I'd do it again if I had to."

"Yes, I'm fairly certain you would," she said, looking at the frozen scene and slowly shaking her head. "You didn't hesitate, even when you were informed you were facing *me*."

"In my defense, up to that point I wasn't exactly running into gods and goddesses," I said. "My case load didn't involve facing down and stopping gods."

"Yet you persisted, why?"

"Monty was alone and outclassed," I said. "Actually, we were *both* outclassed, but I wasn't going to walk away and leave him alone."

"Of course not," she said. "Your sense of self-preservation appears to be non-existent, even now."

"And did I mention the *kids*?"

"Shiva knew exactly how to get you involved," she said. "He did his research well."

"This meeting with the mage was another inflection point," she continued. "Had you refused to take this case, you would have irrevocably altered your path. Yet *you chose* to take the case."

She motioned with her hand and we were outside a warehouse on Laight Street. I remembered it well. It was the building Ramirez had sent us to recon.

I remembered being marked by Shiva.

"Now that you bring this up," I said. "What is it with you gods and marking people?"

"Excuse me?"

"Shiva marked me that day," I said. "Monty said it was so that your attacks would home in on me."

"You used that mark to your advantage," she replied,

looking to the side. "That was not its purpose. The mage was incorrect. Shiva never lets his pawns survive his manipulations."

"He was going to kill me?"

"He was going to kill the both of you."

"Both of us?"

"Yes. After you managed to breach my defenses, his need for you ended," she answered. "You had served your purpose. You were merely a tool."

"He had tricked Monty and duped me."

"You were easy. You were a normal, with no overt knowledge of the supernatural," she added. "Deceiving the mage, however, required levels of subterfuge."

"Monty didn't see the play until it was too late," I realized. "You saved him."

"That was the arrangement, yes."

"Arrangement? Arrangement with who?"

"Whom, and that is not for me to share."

"It was over for us in that warehouse," I said. "It was supposed to be our last night."

"For the both of you, yes," she said. "*You chose* to confront Shiva, a god. Even when you knew your life was forfeit, you remained and faced death."

"It's not like I could've walked away," I said. "You had beat me into the ground by then. Not that I was much of a threat."

"The damage had been done," she said. "You forced my hand into destroying my Rakshasa. I underestimated your...*resilience and tenacity*."

"And I your ruthlessness."

"I do try," she said with a small bow. "Now focus on this part and we will put this matter to rest, once and for all."

She waved her hand and the scene shifted again.

Shiva had entered the warehouse.

He explained how he had used Monty and me, how he was the one stealing the children and trying to drain their life-force. Now he was moving to his endgame.

He had gathered green orbs of energy and was flinging them around like party favors.

I saw myself fire twice, hitting him in the chest. He released the orb he held and shattered me.

I should've died then.

Then Kali stepped close to me.

"Today, I curse you with life," she said, and grabbed my left hand.

She placed the pendant she held on it, as white light shot out from her hand into mine. The pendant disappeared, and my left hand burst into white flame.

I reflexively looked down and rubbed my mark.

"Your third inflection point of this encounter," she said, pointing. "I had healed you by this point."

"You also had *cursed* me."

"The two were one and the same," she said. "There needed to be a consequence to your actions. I could have let you die."

"I remember, you said you couldn't touch the mage, but you would give me something far worse," I said, as the memory rushed back. "Why couldn't you touch Monty?"

"Why don't you ask *him*?"

"Because he probably doesn't know," I said. "It's how divine beings operate. Everything important you say is all cryptic and shrouded in shadow. If I ask him, he'll be like: 'I have no bloody clue. Did she tell you to ask me? Were those her exact words?' In his typical mage response."

"He has the answer if he knows how to look."

"See? That's exactly what I mean," I said, aware she wasn't going to give me a straight answer. "Where was the consequence to *his* actions?"

"Now you are asking the right questions, but I still cannot give you that answer," she said. "That answer is not mine to share."

I shook my head and turned back to the scene.

I saw Shiva blast me into oblivion. I collapsed from his attack, bloody and battered, on the verge of death.

"I should have died there," I said, pointing at the broken me. "Then you cursed me alive."

"Yet despite my curse, you chose to stay and face death yet again."

"No god is safe," I said. "I learned that lesson."

"It still holds true."

"You *threw* me at Shiva," I said, remembering how she flung me across the floor. I remembered crashing through his shields and the concussive blast destroying the building when I slammed into Shiva. "You *used* me as a weapon."

"I still do," she said matter-of-factly, as the scene slowly dematerialized and we were standing in the temple courtyard again. "Only not so literally these days."

"You're right," I said after the scene completely vanished. "Three times I had the chance to walk away. Well, that last time I wasn't walking away anywhere, because Shiva wanted to disintegrate me, but I get it. I had more than one chance to walk away."

"No longer," she said. "You are my Marked One, the Aspis, among other things."

I nodded.

"Are you ready?" she asked.

"No, but that never stopped me before."

"Good," she said. "Prepare."

FOUR

I was still leaning against one of the three walls that surrounded the temple. She was standing several feet away when I caught her movement.

It was only a twitch, a slight shift of her bodyweight, but it was enough to set off all the alarms in my head. My body moved without waiting for my conscious instruction.

That reflex saved my life.

By the time she slid at me, I was on the courtyard floor, rolling away. She continued past me and put her fist through the temple wall, shattering a piece of the thick wall to rubble.

I kept rolling and got to my feet.

I held up a hand and she stood still.

I was shocked that had worked, but quickly recovered and pointed at the wall indignantly.

"That would've *killed* me," I said, giving her an accusing look. "You would have taken my head off. Is that what we're doing here?"

She glanced at the destroyed section of the wall, and then looked back at me with a small smile on her lips.

"Why did you think I brought you here?" she asked,

putting one hand on her hip. "To reminisce and discuss how *you* ruined my five-thousand-year-old plan?"

Ouch.

I winced.

"I didn't know this was supposed to be a survival exercise," I said. "Why not do this at the school?"

"There's no one here to rescue you, if I do choose to kill you," she said with a shrug. "Your life is mine. Don't you understand that by now?"

"My life is yours?"

She crossed her arms and stared at me. Her eyes flared with a brief flash of violet energy. The air around me suddenly dropped a few degrees in temperature, reminding me that she didn't need to *actually* hit me to cause life-ending damage.

"You disagree?"

I shook my head

"Not contradicting," I said, raising a hand in surrender. "Just getting used to the idea."

"You should have 'gotten used to the idea' long ago," she said. "Now. Form a shield."

"Form a shield?" I asked, looking around. "Why would I need to form a shield?"

She jumped in the air.

"What?" I yelled, looking up as she gained altitude. "What are you doing?"

"Form a shield," her voice drifted down to where I stood. "Or not. Your choice."

My brain barely had time to process what was happening. It looked oddly familiar, then I realized where I had seen this move before.

She floated in the air above me, looked down and gave me a smile.

It was not a warm smile.

It was the smile of impending death.

She's really doing this? What the hell?

She hovered in the air for a few seconds, and slowly did a pirouette. At the apex, she turned her body like an Olympic diver. She extended an arm and closed her hand, aiming herself at me, fist-first.

A phoenix fist. A Kali-powered phoenix fist. I'm so dead.

My brain seized in that moment for several reasons: She was unleashing a variation of Nana's phoenix fist. I was currently at ground zero. There was no way I could form a shield strong enough to withstand a phoenix fist from Nana, much less one from Kali.

She is going to kill me.

The next thought that raced through my mind was: *you could run.*

I even looked around for half a second before forgetting that idea. If this was a real phoenix fist, I couldn't run away fast enough or far enough to escape the blast.

My only hope was in my dawnward.

I looked up again, wasting a precious second to try and figure out her angle of attack, and noticed her hand was glowing a deep violet.

That can't be good.

I focused.

For another brief second I considered using my mark, then realized how futile that would be. Kali was the one who had burned the mark into my hand. I doubted using it at this moment was going to have any beneficial effect.

I focused and let the energy surge within me as I formed a dawnward. The dome of violet energy formed around me. I made it smaller than usual, about five feet in diameter, trying to compress the actual dome into a compact area of protection.

I tried to force more energy into the dawnward, offering me what little protection I had from Kali's phoenix fist.

I realized in that moment that I should have invested some time to study how to make a dawnward more thoroughly. It was clear that my knowledge on the making of protective energy was lacking.

There is no way I'm surviving this.

I felt her energy signature from where I stood, and she was still in the air and heading my way. Once that energy hit my dawnward, she would disintegrate it and me.

Kali crashed into my dawnward and the world exploded in violet light. Rather than be blown apart into small Simon bits, Kali, who had landed, grabbed my wrist, and held me in place as the temple exploded around us.

I looked around in awe as the stone splintered and shattered into rubble as the destructive force from her fist exploded outward. After a few seconds, realizing my dawnward had been blown away in the first half-second, I saw *her* protective shield had deflected all of the destructive energy away from us.

She had unleashed a phoenix fist and a dawnward to counter its effects, all at the same time.

"Your dawnward is lacking, *Aspis*," she said, giving me a look of disdain with the last word. "How have you managed to protect *anything* with that sad excuse of a shield?"

She paused, waved a hand and repaired the damage from her fist.

"I'm not going around fighting gods," I said. "My dawnward is not rated to withstand divine phoenix fists."

"Rated?" she said, glancing at me as the destruction began to calm. "Your dawnward can barely stop a hard look."

"I'm still new to most of this."

"That is a poor excuse," she said, waving my words away. "Do you think your enemies—*my* enemies—will extend you the courtesy of compassionate understanding?"

"I have noticed a certain lack of understanding by those

willing to shred me to death," I said. "Why are your enemies also my enemies? I get your enemies by proxy?"

"Yes. You don't just get the benefits of being my Marked One, you get the consequences too," she said. "Do you know what I have noticed?"

"What?"

"All I have noticed is my Marked One running from successors and creating weak shields," she said. "You are the Marked of *Kali*. You are *my* Aspis, not the designated victim. The Marked of *Kali* is meant to instill fear and terror in their enemies by their mere presence."

"You don't think I instill fear?" I asked, staring at her. "My presence is pretty intimidating."

"To whom?" she asked, staring back. "Who actually fears you? Who hears your name being mentioned and shudders with the anticipation of crossing your path or facing your wrath? Show me this pathetic creature."

"Fine, I'm not making anyone shudder with terror at crossing my path—yet," I said, holding up a finger. "But I *can* be intimidating."

"No," she said, shaking her head. "Intimidating is not the first thing that comes to mind when I think of you."

"Maybe it's time for a new era of the Marked of Kali, a kinder and gentler era?" I said. "Not one filled with terror, death and maiming?"

She cocked her head to one side while fixing me with a piercing glare. I wanted to run, but my legs had decided to ignore all the signals from my brain in that moment.

"I am Kali," she said, her voice a promise of pain and mangling. "In this form, terror, death, and maiming are the expected instruments I use to convey my wishes and desires."

"I was just saying—"

"Not only do I fill my worshippers with fear, other gods,

other *pantheons* hear my name and pause. I am the Destroyer."

"I get that," I said, realizing there was a good chance I ended this conversation as a pile of dust. "It could be that only applies to you?"

She sighed, and I could almost see her counting to ten.

"Strong, as the Marked of Kali you are an extension of me. It is why you bear my mark. You *must* convey the same presence."

"Maybe, hear me out," I said, raising a hand. "Is it possible your mark didn't take? Maybe it needs several applications?"

She moved faster than my senses could register and tapped me in the forehead with a finger. I flew across the courtyard and bounced off the statue of Nandi; to be more specific, I slammed into the bull's ass and caromed into one of the intact walls, which mercilessly remained still as I broke a few ribs in the collision.

I crumpled to the ground as my curse kicked in, blasting my body with inferno-like heat. In moments, I was as good as new but the pain, the pain stayed with me.

Somehow, I knew she was doing this intentionally.

She walked over to where I lay and looked down at me.

FIVE

"Looks like my mark is completely intact," she said, pointing at my forehead. "Would you like me to try the reapplication again? I can make it more forceful this time, though I doubt you would survive *that* process."

"No," I said, quickly getting to my feet and gingerly touching my forehead. "You know, now that I sit with it for a moment, I can feel the full effect of your mark even now. It's a tingling effect, like a cluster migraine and a gentle, excruciating stabbing pain in both of my eyes. I'm sure it took this time."

She raised a finger.

"I'm willing to try again if you doubt the efficacy of my methods," she said in a gentle voice and with a warm smile that drove a cold spike of fear into my heart. "As many times as it takes."

"No, really," I said, taking a futile step back, as if I could escape her. "There's really no need."

She waved her hand again and formed a long, ornate stone bench. She motioned for me to sit. I sat as far as possible from her as I could physically manage.

She gestured and formed two mugs.

Mine appeared by my side, and I could smell the potent coffee. Her mug held some green liquid that gave off a subtle glow.

She sipped from her mug and looked at me.

"Death Wish extra strong," she said, looking at the steaming mug next to me. "Never a bad time for coffee"—she raised her mug in my direction—"or tea."

"I've never seen glowing green tea before," I said, reaching for my mug. "You really made Death Wish?"

"Yes," she said. "I'm sure by now there are plenty of things that you have seen that can fall under the category of things you never expected to see in your life."

"True," I said, taking a sip of my coffee and experiencing some of the best javambrosia I had ever tasted. "This is amazing."

She nodded in my direction.

"Thank you," she said. "Ever since that night at the warehouse, where you interrupted my plans, you have been living through an extended grace period."

"A grace period?"

"You were human, inexperienced, and unaccustomed to the supernatural world," she said before taking another sip. "That afforded you a certain grace. That grace period is coming to a swift end."

"I've realized the caliber of enemies has increased in lethality," I said, thinking about Caligo and her master, Rakta. "There are several players in the shadows."

"Some of whom are stepping into the light."

"Like Caligo?"

She nodded again, but looked across the courtyard.

"Caligo is merely a pawn," she said, looking down into her mug. "A dangerous pawn, but still a piece to be moved about at the whims of her master. He is the real threat."

"Will we be able to face Rakta?"

"You are my Marked. Eventually you will—you must," she answered. "The question is will you survive that meeting. Right now, you are not ready to face a demon of that caliber."

"That sounds encouraging."

Then I realized what she was doing.

If she had told me I wasn't ready for the Grand Council, I may not have believed her out of sheer stubbornness. What she was doing, was *showing* me how unprepared I was.

She smiled without looking in my direction.

"You have no idea the level of the enemies that are gathering to bring about your destruction," she said, looking at the statue of Nandi. "If they manage to get hold of you as you are now,"—she glanced at me—"your death is certain. Worse, in your present state, you can't protect those you care for."

"They're not just coming for *me*, are they?"

"Of course not," she said. "You know how this works. They'll kill everyone you know, and everyone they know, until you are alone. Then, and only then, when you are in the depths of rage and despair, will they come for you."

"This is like some twisted supernatural mafia family with a vendetta against me," I said. "There's no way to stop them?"

"There is."

"There is?" I asked, surprised. "No one informed me."

"There is no need to *inform* you," she said. "You know the way." She looked at me as violet energy flashed across her eyes again. "It's quite simple—and final."

"I mean without killing an entire army of angry supernaturals."

She shook her head and glanced away again.

"Violence, mind-rending violence, is the currency of my world," she said. "It's the only language my enemies speak. I suggest you become fluent in its use."

"What about tact?" I asked, hoping against hope. "No chance of using diplomacy?"

"How has that worked for you in the past?" she asked. "Have your attempts at tact served you or your mage?"

"Not really, no," I admitted. "Most of the enemies we face are holding major amounts of pent-up rage. Tact doesn't bring out the best in rage-filled creatures."

"My enemies are not the negotiating type," she replied, looking down at the subtle green glow in her cup again. "They won't just kill you outright. They will capture the mage, followed by your hellhound, and everyone your life touches. They will torture them and make you watch. Once they have died the hardest death you will have witnessed in your life, they will focus on you. If you are not going to take this seriously, I may as well slit your throat now and save you the agony."

"You really know how to make enemies."

"It's a gift, born in hatred and envy."

"I'm becoming familiar with it."

"If you like, I could show you how it would end for those you care about," she offered. "I've heard a picture is worth a thousand words."

"No. That won't be necessary," I said. "The last time you did that is still fresh in my memory. Pass."

"I understand," she said with a short nod. "You need to comprehend that my enemies are your enemies as well."

I gave her statement some thought.

"I know beings with power," I said after a pause. "I can call on them to help me and mine."

She nodded.

"You could," she said. "Some would answer the call, even to the point of risking their lives for you and the mage. I daresay, Dexter Montague and others would risk their lives for you, Tristan, and your hound."

"Sounds like there is a huge but at the end of that sentence."

"Would you want them to?"

"I don't follow," I said. "I would need help. Actually, I already do *need* the help. If they called on me, I wouldn't hesitate to help them."

"This world you move in now doesn't operate like the one you are accustomed to," she said, then took another sip. "Offering help can do more harm than good in most cases."

"What?" I said. "How does *that* make any sense?"

She sighed.

"I occasionally forget how young and inexperienced you are," she said. "Let me explain this in simple terms you would understand."

"Please. I'd appreciate that."

"Let's say you call on Dexter to assist you to deal with my enemies," she said. "A reasonable request; he is powerful and closely connected to you. It stands to reason you would make this request and it seems straightforward."

"Yes," I said. "Dex can pulverize the enemies trying to erase me. He's strong enough to do it without breaking a sweat."

"Except that the enemies that are now taking notice of you also know powerful beings, beings that are strong enough to stand against Dexter and hold their own."

"Caligo?"

She shook her head.

"Rakta, and other demons stronger than him."

She paused to let the words sink in.

I had never considered that there were other beings just as strong or stronger than Dex. That was naive and foolish. Of course there were beings stronger than Dex out there.

"That would be bad."

"No, remove the morality from the equation," she said.

"This is not about good or bad. It's a matter of the equivalence of force and power. They would merely be matching the forces you have arrayed."

"Still sounds bad."

"For you, perhaps," she answered. "Not so bad for them."

"Having to fight against anyone or anything as strong as Dex would be bad for me," I said. "Do you know how powerful Dex is?"

"I am *acutely* aware of his level of power. Most divine beings that interact with this plane are aware of the power Dexter Montague wields, and his potential," she said. "What do you think that means?"

"He's extremely powerful."

"And?"

"Knowing Dex, he has a buttload of enemies."

"A buttload?" she asked. "That is an odd form of measurement, but it can apply. He has an extreme amount of enemies, disproportionate to his age."

"I don't understand."

"Dexter Montague has enemies worthy of a divine being," she clarified. "He hasn't lived nearly long enough to justify the number or caliber of his enemies, yet their hate for him burns like the heart of a sun. He also has one significant liability."

"He underdresses?" I volunteered. "I mean he could stand to invest in more clothing."

She stared at me and I felt the energy around me increase slightly. She took another sip and sighed as she glanced at me.

"Just when I think you are comprehending the gravity of your situation, you utter something completely ridiculous."

I became serious.

"Sorry," I said. "It's reflex. This weakness—is it that he's mortal?"

She stared at me again, this time with some reluctant respect.

"Correct," she said after a moment. "Even though he bears the mantle of the Harbinger, Dexter Montague *can* die. Now, knowing this, extrapolate the rest."

"That's not much information."

"Strong, don't insult my intelligence, I know what you are capable of and what you do to mask fear and uncertainty. Extrapolate the rest. You are in mortal danger."

"I'm in trouble, I call on Dex to help," I said, putting the scenario together in my head. "He comes to help, but your enemies anticipate that, and call on some being, Super Mage McKickass that's just as, or stronger, than Dex."

"What does that do?"

"It basically neutralizes Dex by keeping him busy," I said. "Now Dex is tied up with this Mage who is powerful, while also trying to figure out how to help me."

"What does his *buttload* of enemies do?"

"Oh hell, that would be the perfect time to ambush him," I said. "His attention is divided, he's focused on keeping me and probably Monty alive. They will attack him and us in an effort to get him to drop his guard."

"I believe the Grand Council is currently employing this strategy," she said. "He outplayed them by passing the mantle of Harbinger to his nephew, but that won't work indefinitely. He will have to make a choice soon."

"The Grand Council wanted to draw him into the conflict?"

"They still do," she said. "And at this point in your scenario, you have managed to spark a conflict so large that it is beyond you. A conflict that could lead to a major war among the ranks of beings that could obliterate entire planes with their battles."

"That's why he tries to avoid our conflicts."

"He doesn't avoid them, he mitigates them," she said. "Many times he is acting before you even know there is a conflict. The Harbinger has much influence and leverage, but even that has its limits."

"That explains his emphasizing our getting stronger," I said. "He can't fight our battles without causing ripples."

"Ripples is a quaint way of describing it," she said. "Consider it more like a tsunami effect of destruction. Have I made myself clear?"

"Yes, but I wasn't born into this life," I said. "I'm still new to all of this."

She waved my words away.

"That time has passed," she said. "You are not *new* to this any longer and it's time you accepted who and what you are. Not just the words. I mean you must accept the responsibility that comes with the titles."

"I can barely wrap my head around your curse," I countered. "I'm just supposed to accept—?"

"Yes, Simon," she said, cutting me off. "You don't have the luxury to be lax about this. The time for excuses has passed. My enemies will show you no mercy. To cause you pain is to strike at me. Don't you understand? They won't come at me. They can't, not directly, but they *will* come for you—repeatedly. Because they can."

"I didn't ask to be—"

She raised an eyebrow and silenced me.

"I thought we established this?"

"My apologies, I did ask for this," I said, recognizing how close I was to being blasted to tiny Simon particles, not by a phoenix fist, but by her bad mood. "How do you expect a human to deal with a phoenix fist or any attack from your enemies? That's insane. This whole situation is insane."

She looked off at Nandi again and took a long pull from her still steaming mug of glowing green tea. After a few moments, she placed her mug down, but remained looking at the statue of Shiva in the central shrine.

"Are you calling *me* insane?" she asked, softly. "Are you questioning my judgment?"

The words hung between us.

I may have been crazy, but I wasn't *that* crazy. I was still firmly in the 'enjoying breathing and having all my limbs attached' club, and enjoyed my membership there.

Her question definitely came with a not-so-thinly veiled promise of obliteration. It always surprised me how those who were of questionable mental stability were the most touchy about it.

I decided a new strategy was needed—tact.

"I'm calling the expectation unrealistic."

She answered with a short nod, took another sip, and looked at me.

"Let's assess, shall we?"

I didn't like where this was going.

"Assess? Sure," I said. "Sounds relatively pain-free."

"You are cursed alive, yes?"

"Yes," I said warily, concerned where this was going. "Because you cursed me?"

"You are an Aspis, not a very good one, but an Aspis nonetheless, yes?"

"Yes."

"You are bonded to a hellhound, correct?"

"Yes," I said. "You do realize I was gifted Peaches. It's not like I went to an infernal pet store and picked up the hellhound in the window."

"Did you accept the gift?"

"Yes."

"You wield a blade that should have killed you several iterations ago; your vampire is playing a dangerous game, but that is a discussion for another time. As far I can see," she glanced at my chest, "this weapon you possess is a seraphic blade, which is also a necrotic siphon. Have I correctly determined most of its properties?"

"Yes, you have," I said then caught myself. "*Most* of its properties?"

"Yes, most. You also possess the ability to manipulate energy, though you are not a mage," she continued, ignoring my questioning tone. "You have a cast you call a magic missile, do you not? Where you utilize your life-force to create a blast of energy, among other things, yes?"

I knew better than to push it. If she had wanted to go there, she would have. It would have to be a topic for another time.

"Yes, I do."

"Tell me then, *Aspis*, in your considerably short life, how many humans have you encountered that possess all these qualities to the extent that you do?"

I paused and gave it some real thought.

I had met plenty of people who had some of these qualities—mages could manipulate energy, Hades was a bondmate to Cerberus, and Grey wielded the sentient Darkspirit blade which was the pair to Ebonsoul.

They all had some of the qualities, but none of them possessed all of the qualities.

Like I did.

I was about to answer, when she raised her finger, silencing me.

"Consider this further," she said, standing. "What makes you think you are still entirely human?"

That question stunned me into silence.

"What do you mean?" I asked after a moment. "Are you saying I'm not human?"

"You tell me," she said, stepping near Nandi the bull statue, as she repaired the rest of the temple grounds with a wave of her hand. "How many humans can do what you do?"

"There are plenty of mages out there that can do some amazing things," I said. "What about them?"

"Mages *are* technically human, except that their lifespans are quite extended and that they have, through rigorous training, managed to unlock methodologies that allow for the manipulation of the fundamental principles of energy that underpin the very planes of existence. Just like every other normal human you've known, yes?"

She had made her point.

"But they are *mostly* human."

"Mostly human is also slightly inhuman."

I stared at her in disbelief.

"Did you just Miracle Max me?"

"I have no idea who you are referring to," she said with a slight smile. "Do you know any mage, or person, for that matter, that is currently bonded to a hellhound?" she asked. "In fact the only other person I know bonded to a hellhound is a god. Do you know of another?"

"No," I said. "What about the Midnight Echelon?"

She gave me a look that said: *really?*

"The Midnight Echelon is comprised of Dark Valkyries," she said, shaking her head. "Even among the Valkyries, the Echelon is singular. There is a reason they hold the position that they do. You have seen them in battle—they are not to be trifled with. Do they come across as 'human' to you?"

"Not in a thousand years."

She nodded.

"Some even longer."

"You want me to accept that I'm not entirely human," I said, looking at the newly repaired temple courtyard. It shouldn't have been difficult considering I was speaking to a goddess, while standing on some strange plane. "Easier said than done."

"Perhaps this reluctance is what you are using as a

crutch," she said. "If you can remain in the realm of disbelief, you can cling to your 'humanity' while shirking the burden only *you* can carry."

Her words stung, but rung of the truth.

"I'm not shirking anything."

"Prove it."

"How do I even *prove* something like that?"

"The next time we meet, I *will* kill you. Unless you can stop me."

"Stop you?" I said incredulously. "I can't face a goddess."

"While true, in this incarnation"—she swept a hand across her body—"if you had an adequate shield, you could withstand my attack," she said. "As it stands now, your shield is about as effective as a deep thought."

"How do I make it stronger?" I asked, crushing any ego I might've had about my skill. "How do I learn?"

She paused and stared at me for a few moments, then nodded in approval.

"Why didn't you ask me to increase your power?" she asked. "Several of my previous Marked have made this request."

"Did you fulfill it?"

"No, never," she answered. "The Marked of Kali must learn to tap into the power of the mark they bear. Without any assistance from me. To assist you would negate the purpose of the mark."

"I always did figure you for a DIY goddess," I said with a nod. "No offense, but you're not exactly the 'come to my rescue' type."

"I am not."

"That's why I didn't ask you for help."

"Good," she said. "I know that request cost you. Because you asked, I will provide you the direction you need."

"I do appreciate it."

"Go find the ancient mage called the Spartan. He can help you with your shield and increasing your power. I suggest you do so with haste, before the Grand Council unleashes more Magistrates to deal with you and your mage. Even now, they dispatch enemies to eliminate you both."

"Who is this Spartan?" I asked. "Is that his name? Really?

"I didn't say it was his name, I said that was what he was called."

"How do I find him?"

She gave me a look and shook her head.

"The clue to his location is in his name."

"What do you mean, the Grand Council is dispatching more enemies?" I asked, as my brain caught up to her words. "I thought we—?"

"You thought what, exactly? That they would just take their defeat quietly and leave you alone?" she asked. "All you have done in thwarting their intentions, is pushed them to redouble their efforts."

"They came after us."

"Yes, and you humiliated them," she said with a smile. "Well done. I expect no less from my Marked."

"Well done? You just said they are sending *more* Magistrates after us," I said. "How is that well done?"

"You have improved the caliber of your enemies," she said. "I approve. However, make no mistake, they have not forgotten, nor will they forgive. They will come for you all." She looked off to the side as all the Rakshasa reappeared in the courtyard. My hellhound bounded out from behind one of the walls and came to my side. She patted him on the head, rubbing behind his ears as he chuffed. "You must grow stronger before you face the Grand Council. Our time has concluded, for now."

She gave me a look, turned, and started walking away. She

pointed to one of the walls and a portal formed. Through it, I could see the Battlemagic school grounds.

"I suggest you speak to the old man," she said, slowly fading from view. "He may have the answers you need. Do not tarry, Aspis. Time works for you, but it also works against you."

She disappeared a second later.

I ran through the portal and found myself in the courtyard of the Montague School of Battlemagic.

SIX

I arrived in the courtyard with Monty heading my way.

Next to me, I felt my hellhound ram into my legs, tangling himself in between my knees, and bringing me crashing down to the ground in a spectacular takedown.

He managed to unpretzel himself with ease, and made a dash for the courtyard exit as Cece and Peanut ran into the courtyard ahead of Monty, chasing after Peaches.

I slowly got to my feet as Monty approached, looking after my hellhound and the girls running away.

"You survived your visit," he said, giving me a once-over. "Well done."

"Barely survived," I said. "She obliterated my dawnward with a phoenix fist."

"An actual phoenix fist?" he said, raising an eyebrow. "And you're alive to tell the tale? She must have handicapped her power. A true phoenix fist from a goddess like Kali would have rendered you to a distant memory, despite your curse."

"I had a feeling she was holding back," I said, dusting myself off. "She did promise to kill me the next time we meet. So there's that."

He nodded.

"How pleasant. I take it she was displeased with your dawnward demonstration?'

"You could say that," I said as we crossed the courtyard and headed to one of the larger buildings. "Called it *lacking*."

"I see. Did she provide any guidance on how you could improve its efficacy?" he asked. "Anything that someone without mage qualities could learn?"

"You could just say I'm not a mage," I said. "I'm not going to get offended. It's the truth."

"I thought I did," he answered. "Well, did she?"

"She said I need to go to Sparta," I said, then paused. "No, that's not exactly right. There was a lot going on."

"Was she giving you historical lessons?"

"No, she was busy bouncing me around the temple grounds."

"When she suddenly decided to discuss Ancient Greece?" Monty asked, rubbing his chin. "That sounds suspect, considering our next objective. We do need to locate Ichnaea, or Themis, as she is more commonly known. Greece would be the most logical starting point."

"We're going to have to put Themis on hold," I said. "We need to get stronger first, before we go up against the Grand Council."

"And this needs to happen in Greece?"

"She did say something about Sparta," I said. "Give me a sec. It wasn't exactly Sparta."

"Tell me she didn't say you needed to see the *Spartan*."

"That's it!" I said, raising my voice and pointing at him. "I need to find the mage called the Spartan. Kali said the clue to his location was in his name. I'm guessing he's in Sparta?"

"The Spartan," Monty said, slowly. "Are you certain she said that exact term?"

"Yes, she said in order to increase my shield's power, I

need to go see the mage called the Spartan," I said, looking at him. "You don't look happy. What's wrong?"

"Rumor has it that the Spartan was a hoplite who survived the battle of Thermopylae," Monty said. "No one knows his origins for sure."

"He survived the battle of Thermopylae?" I said. "That would make him—?"

"Over two thousand five hundred years old," Monty said. "The battle occurred in 480BC."

"And he's still alive?" I asked in disbelief. "The same person?"

"As far as anyone knows, yes," Monty said. "What is only known to a select few is his other title—the Hidden Hand."

"The Hidden Hand?" I said. "What does that mean?"

"Exactly what it sounds like," Dex said from behind us as we entered the main building and rounded one of the corners. "The Hidden Hand is a mage few have heard of, and even fewer have met. He prefers it that way."

Dex was carrying a few large binders and actually appeared like an academic. He wore his hair neat, pulled back in a tight ponytail, and held in place by a clip in the form of a green raven. His white linen shirt was buttoned up except for the top two buttons. His dark slacks accentuated the shirt and he looked nearly professional except for the lack of shoes and the toe rings.

I gave him a once-over and nodded.

"Looking respectable there," I said, pointing to the outfit. "Meeting someone?"

"As a matter of fact, I am," he said. "A potential instructor for the school. Mo said I need to make a good impression and dress like a headmaster."

"I think headmasters wear shoes," Monty said, glancing at Dex's feet and raising an eyebrow. "Have you given any consideration to a suit? Headmasters usually wear something a little more formal."

"Never going to happen, nephew," Dex said with a scowl. "Mo's lucky to get me into this much clothing. A suit? With a tie, and shoes? Never. I see you survived your visit with Kali?"

"She wanted to share some concerns," I said. "Like how my shields are lacking."

"Ah," Dex said with a nod. "I see she was making a point about you wearing her mark."

He pointed to my forehead.

"Yes, she was making a point, literally."

"She never was one for subtlety," he said. "She belongs to the old school of training."

"The old school?"

"If it doesn't kill you, it makes you stronger," he said. "A few of her Marked did *not* get stronger."

"She mentioned you by name," I said. "Seems like a few gods know about you."

"Aye," he said with a nod. "I've made an impression or two, along with my share of enemies."

"She did mention that."

"Sounds like you had yourself an interesting conversation," he said, glancing over at Monty. "Why were you two discussing H?"

"H? Doesn't he have an actual name?"

"If he does, no one knows it," Dex said. "He's never shared it with me or anyone I know. I stopped trying to figure it out centuries ago."

"You've *met* him?" I asked. "Face to face?"

"Aye," Dex said. "A few times in some heated battles and complicated intrigues. He likes to be in the mix of what he considers pivotal moments of history."

"How does he know they're pivotal moments?"

"Because he makes them pivotal," Dex said. "Why are ye discussing the Hidden Hand?"

"Kali said I need to find the Spartan before facing the Grand Council," I said. "Monty said the Spartan was also the Hidden Hand."

"As far as I know," Monty answered. "It's the accepted rumor among the older mage sects, though no one will confirm it."

"Because they can't," Dex said with a smile. "The Spartan and H are assumed to be the same mage. I've personally never seen them together."

"That's the proof?" I asked, incredulous. "That they've never been seen together?"

"Did Kali mention why she's sending you to see the Spartan?" Dex asked. "What was her reason?"

"She said that was the best way to increase the strength of my shield," I answered. "She said the Grand Council isn't going to stop coming after us, and we're not strong enough."

"Aye, they're not the type to let this go," he said. "Especially after your last interaction with Emeric. Getting stronger would be an excellent idea."

"She also explained why you can't get more directly involved," I said. "At least, she explained some of it."

He nodded.

"One of the dangers of the Harbinger Mantle," he said. "It gives you a certain freedom, yes, but it also comes with shackles. For me to get directly involved in everything concerning you two would be…problematic."

"'Tsunamis of destruction' were her exact words," I said. "Would it be that bad?"

"Ach," he said, waving my words away. "Kali is being overdramatic. There would be repercussions. Of course. Some of the older gods would take notice—never a good thing. Maybe some ancient demons and beings of power would want a word or two, but nothing so dramatic as a tsunami of destruction."

"I disagree," Monty said, brushing off a sleeve. "Your intervention in our situations would create more than mere repercussions. Case in point, the Grand Council wants to eliminate us because of the actions you took with the Golden Circle."

Dex's expression darkened briefly.

"That's not only because of the Golden Circle and my actions," Dex said, "though I take full credit for what I've done and would do it again if given the chance. No, the Grand Council is moving against you two because of *who* you are, or will be."

"Who we are? I don't understand," I said. "What does that mean?"

Dex looked at his watch and shook his head.

"I'm going to be late, but it can't be helped," he said. "This is important for you two to understand. Who you are—not now, but when you grow into your power, presents a clear threat to those who would prefer to hold onto power."

"That is about as clear as ink," I said. "Can you clarify?"

"Of course," he said. "Then I'll have Mo upset with me for being tardy to this meeting. Which do you think I'll be choosing?"

"Not pissing Mo off?" I guessed. "That would be the safer of the two choices."

"Smart lad," he said and began walking away. "I'll tell you this much—the Grand Council was always going to move against you two. One, because of my nephew's parents, and two, because of who marked you."

"Huh? What?"

"I merely accelerated the inevitable," he said, turning a corner and disappearing from sight. "It's early, but it's safer this way. We'll speak later."

"What did that mean?" I said, turning to Monty. "Did that mean anything to you? Why would it be safer to have the Grand Council after us now?

"I don't think that's what he meant," Monty said, tapping his chin. "I think he meant it's safer to have their machinations uncovered earlier rather than later."

"He said your parents," I said. "Does that include your mom too?"

"I would presume so," Monty said as we headed downstairs to the labs. "That is troubling."

"You've never really mentioned her, why not?" I asked. "I mean if you don't feel comfortable talking about her, I understand. It's your private life."

"My mother is a difficult subject because of who she was," Monty said, pausing as we arrived at the lower level. "She was a powerful magic user who had close associations with Hecate."

"The goddess, Hecate?"

He nodded.

"You could see where that would cause problems in a sect full of mages," he said. "Especially when one of them becomes joined to a woman who, for all intents and purposes is considered dark..."

"Dark?"

"Hecate is associated with night, magic, witchcraft, graves and ghosts, among other things," Monty said. "Most of those subjects aren't what's considered practices of the light—with the exception of magic."

"But you said magic is neither dark nor light," I said. "I remember you saying that. You said it all depends on how it's used."

"I still believe that," he said as we approached a lab door. "That doesn't mean the Elders of the sect held the same view. They branded my mother dark; this caused rifts within the sect. To this day, only my father knows how she truly died."

"But your father is—"

"I know," Monty said. "Which means I may never discover how she died."

"Dex?"

"He doesn't know," Monty said. "Only my father was present and he destroyed any evidence of what happened. I don't know why. None of the surviving Montagues know what happened. I've asked them all."

I nodded.

"I'm sorry I brought it up," I said. "I didn't mean to make you remember bad memories."

"Not at all," he said. "I only have fond memories of my mother. She truly understood me. I only wish I could have spent more time with her, had her longer in my life."

"I understand," I said. "Maybe one day we will uncover what happened?"

"Perhaps, one day," he said, pushing on the door to a lab and opening it. "Right now, we have to focus on remaining alive long enough to deal with the enemies who want to shorten our lives."

"Why are we in this lab?" I asked, looking around. "Also, are we safe here?"

"In the lab?" he asked. "I'd say so."

I gave him a look.

"Safe in the school," I said. "Dex sent us to our plane because the Grand Council was going to pay him a visit here. He said it wouldn't be safe if they found us here."

"I think... after our interaction with Alain, we can safely say they consider us enemies of the Grand Council," he said, closing the door and gesturing. The door sealed with a violet flash. "They will dispatch Magistrates and other Emissaries."

"They have more?"

He gave me a look that said: *what do you think?*

"Of course they have more," I continued. "The Grand Council is stepping into heavy hitters, isn't it?"

"You saw Alain and Emeric, you tell me," he said. "They are several orders of magnitude above us in terms of power. In addition, they command an army."

"An army they consider expendable," I said, remembering the reinforcements on Governor's Island. "They didn't think twice about sending them to their deaths."

"And they won't suddenly grow a conscience and reconsider throwing their lives away in the pursuit of our elimination," he said. "In addition, the five mages of the Grand Council itself are considered to be Archmages."

"How exactly are we supposed to face an Archmage?" I asked. "Not one, but five of them?"

"We grow stronger," he said, gesturing again, causing symbols to form on the walls around us. "We start with the known, then step into the unknown."

I didn't recognize the symbols, but they felt dangerous as I looked at them. I saw Monty gesture again, and the symbols shifted from white and violet to black and red.

"Monty, why did those symbols change color?"

"Read the symbols, Simon," he said, stepping across the room. "Read them."

"You know I don't read runic," I said. "I barely understand half of the things you do with your wiggle-finger moves. You expect me to read these symbols?"

He stood there and crossed his arms, staring at me.

Hard.

"Read them."

"I told you, I don't know how to—"

An orb of violet energy punched me in the chest, knocking me off my feet, and bounced me into the wall. I rolled to the side, recovering fast.

"What the hell, Monty?"

"Read the symbols."

"You know I can't—"

"Can't or won't?"

"What are you saying, that I deliberately refuse to read them?"

"Use your innersight and read them," Monty said, forming another orb. This one was a deeper violet with black energy crackling around it. "Do it."

"That orb is looking kind of nasty," I said, pointing at the orb hovering above his hand. "Why don't you put that thing away before one of us gets hurt, mainly me?"

"I will, once you read those symbols over there," he said, pointing to the wall directly to my right and opposite the door. "You read those symbols, I'll get rid of the orb."

I really looked at the lab this time.

We were standing in a fairly large room.

The floor held an immense circle that extended from wall to wall. Inside the circle I saw symbols of all kinds, going in every direction. The circle was carved into the stone floor, which surprised me. Usually these circles were drawn into the floors, which were wood.

I never recalled a lab with a stone floor and a carved circle before stepping into this room.

"What kind of lab is this?" I asked, still looking around. "Since when did we start using stone floors and carved circles? You expect the students to use this lab?"

"This isn't a lab for the students," Monty said. "Stop stalling. Have you deciphered the symbols?"

"You know I haven't," I said with a scowl. "I don't read—"

He released the orb in my direction.

Released wasn't exactly accurate, it was more like he unleashed the orb. He motioned with his hand and the orb leapt from his palm and raced at me like a hungry predator spotting its prey.

I reflexively held up a hand and formed a wall of energy. A section of my dawnward appeared between us. I knew I wasn't strong enough to stop the orb of pain headed my way, so I angled the wall of energy to deflect it away from me.

The orb hit my shield and bounced away, punching into the wall on my left. A second later it exploded, blasting a hole in the wall. The runes on the floor gave off a golden glow and the crater disappeared as the wall repaired itself.

In seconds, it was as good as new.

I glared at Monty.

He had three more orbs floating around him.

"This is not funny," I said. "Put those things away. If Peaches finds out you're trying to hurt me, he's going to put a chomping on you in the worst way. You know that."

Monty gave me a slight smile.

"I have several contingencies in place," he said, motioning to the runes inscribed in the floor. "The runes in this circle effectively hide us from everything, even your hellhound."

"I call BS," I said, getting angrier by the second. "Peaches and I are bonded. These runes can't block our bond."

"Be my guest," Monty said, extending a hand to the runes on the floor. "Call him."

<Hey, boy. Come find me.>

Silence.

I called him again, and he didn't answer or appear.

"Call him louder, maybe your thoughts are too soft?" he said when Peaches didn't appear. "No? Nothing?"

"You know it's not working."

"I told you it wouldn't. In addition, my accomplices—"

"Your accomplices?"

"Cece and Peanut have been instructed to keep him occupied and focused on the love of his life," he said. "That being said, Cece's guardian is currently joining them in touring the new bondmate and familiars area my uncle added to the school grounds."

I gave him a massive dose of stink-eye.

"That is low," I said. "You got the girls involved in whatever this is?"

"Yes," he said. "My final contingency is my most effective. The Morrigan created several pounds of Ezra's pastrami to be rationed out to your hound as long as he remains with my accomplices."

"You involved the Morrigan?"

He nodded.

"Why would Peaches come to your rescue? He can't hear you, and has no reason to fear for your safety. He will remain blissfully unaware of your current situation, basking in the glow of Ragnarok's presence, touring the space specifically designed for him, and enjoying a nearly unlimited supply of his favorite meat. He will not be 'putting a chomping' on anything except the copious amounts of meat I have provided for him."

"I can't believe you," I said. "This is beyond low, Monty."

"I initially disagreed to enact this plan," Monty said. "But I was there when you faced Alain. I saw you wield the darkflame. I saw you transform into a battleform with your hound and become one with him."

"What are you talking about?"

"Your fear is holding you back, and that is going to get us killed," he said. "There is nothing wrong with feeling fear. Fear is a reaction. Courage is a decision. What is yours?"

He launched the three orbs at me.

The first one slammed into my shoulder, shoving me sideways into the wall. It felt as if my arm had been set on fire. The second orb raced at my head. I managed to duck in time, but only just. This set me up for the third orb, which he delayed and sent at me only after the first two had gotten me into position.

The third orb crashed into my chest like a truck and lifted me off my feet, slamming me into the wall. It bounced off the ceiling, leaving a small crater where it impacted, and descended at speed, looking to finish the job by flattening me into the floor.

I rolled to the side and tapped into my power as the orb followed me.

"*Mors Ignis*," I whispered, as I formed Ebonsoul and slashed at the incoming orb. "*Dividere*."

A semicircular blast of black energy cut through the orb, sending the halves to either side of me as they impacted the wall behind me.

Monty stared at me and pointed to the symbols on the wall.

"Read them."

I looked at the wall and unleashed my innersight. At first, the symbols were still a jumble of indecipherable lines. Slowly they started making sense.

The symbols read:

The Deathless must be the Aspis between the oncoming destruction and life. Stand firm, Marked One, for much is expected of you.

Monty nodded.

"We have surmounted all the perils and endured all the agonies of the past. We shall provide against and thus prevail over the dangers and problems of the future, withhold no sacrifice, grudge no toil, seek no sordid gain, fear no foe. All will be well. We have, I believe, within us the life-strength and guiding light by which the tormented world around us may find the harbor of safety after a storm-beaten voyage."

"British bulldogging me twice in row? I'm impressed."

"Not as impressed as I am."

"You knew I could read it?"

"I knew you could read it *and* neutralize the orbs," he said. "Quite effectively, I might add."

"What if I hadn't neutralized the orbs?"

"It was either that or be sent to the infirmary," he said. "Your inherent talents only seem to surface under duress. So I applied an extensive amount of duress. It seems to have worked."

I looked down at Ebonsoul in my hand. With a thought, it became a silver mist and vanished as I absorbed it.

"Did you really do all that with Peaches?"

"Yes," he said. "We're only just beginning, Simon. Kali explained this to you. You are the shield. In every scenario, if you fall, we all fall. You are the lynchpin."

"You are all stronger than I am."

"This is not about strength," he said. "This is about embracing the power you have. This is as much mental as it is physical."

He formed another set of orbs, six this time.

"Feel free to use every tool at your disposal to defend yourself," he continued. "Are you ready?"

I formed Ebonsoul again and nodded.

"Bring it."

SEVEN

I don't know how long we spent in that lab of torture.

It could have been hours, days, or weeks.

Most of the time, Monty succeeded in smashing me with some of his orbs. There were a few times when I managed to escape them or cut them to pieces. I realized the darkflame was stronger than any other flame I had used in the past, but it was taking a toll.

It was powerful, but it was slowly making me tired.

I didn't know if it was using the darkflame so often in such a short time, or the nature of the darkflame itself. What I did know was that it was taking a toll on me. My reaction times were getting slower, some of my defenses were sloppy, and more and more of Monty's orbs were finding their mark.

A few times I had to struggle to keep Ebonsoul from becoming silver mist against my will. I caught myself a few times making an extra effort to stay focused.

Each time, Monty would increase the speed of the orbs or radically change the angles of attack. After that first time, it was never just one orb.

He would unleash swarms at me, making them break off

at weird angles before dive bombing me from behind or out of my blindspots.

Each time I had to rely more on what I could sense than what I could see. After getting pummeled more times than I could count, I could begin to 'see' where his orbs were without having to actually see them visually.

It didn't completely prevent me from getting hit by the orbs, but at least I knew where the attacks were coming from. That helped me brace for the impacts, even if I couldn't entirely avoid them.

"You need to focus harder," Monty said as he prepped another one of this orb swarms. "Stop relying on your vision. Use the energy from Ebonsoul for more than just slashing; let the energy in the blade flow through you."

"If you tell me to 'let go of my conscious self and act on instinct', I'm going to stab you."

"I'd never say something like that, though I do think you should stretch out with your senses," he said, and I could almost see the hint of a smile, or I was just delusional from the constant orb attacks. "Stop confining yourself to just this lab. Tap into the energy inside of you. Channel it through your blade; don't react, anticipate."

"How am I supposed to anticipate something you haven't done yet?" I said, glaring at him. "I'm supposed to read your mind?"

"Not my mind, my intention," he said, gesturing and setting the orbs next to him into lazy orbits around him. I counted at least five of them. They all looked dangerous and painful. "Close your eyes and take a deep breath."

I glared at him warily.

"I won't release them until you tell me you're ready," he continued. "Mind you, you'll get no such consideration from our enemies. I don't seem to recall any of the creatures we've faced asking if we were ready before trying to execute us."

"Good point."

"But in the spirit of furthering your progress, let's attempt it this way," he said. "Say when."

I closed my eyes and focused.

I slowed my breath and felt the energy in and around me, flowing in a loop starting in my center and traveling throughout my body. It would flow outward, through me and travel into Ebonsoul before returning back to my body.

"You feel it?" Monty asked. "You can sense the flow?"

I nodded.

"Yes," I said, holding Ebonsoul in front of me as I entered a defensive stance. "I can feel it."

"Good, ready?"

I took a few more breaths before nodding.

"As ready as I'm ever going to be."

"Keep your eyes closed," he said. "You can't depend on sight, it's too slow. See without seeing."

I nodded again and he released the orbs.

The first orb shot forward, heading for my face. I almost gave him a glare, but that would have ended with an orb punching me in my face. I slipped to the side and moved my head, avoiding the first orb.

I remained wary, in case it was one of those boomerang orbs that would fly past and then circle back to smack me in the back of my head.

It wasn't.

I felt it punch into the wall behind me and heard the crunch as it buried itself into the stone. He would unleash two more next. I didn't know how I knew, but I just knew.

I felt them before they were close and slashed at the air in front of me. I knew he would aim for my chest. The energy from Ebonsoul intercepted the two orbs, destroying them before they got close.

I took a moment to gloat.

It was a mistake.

In that split-second of diverted focus, as I admired how awesome I was, he added another orb and unleashed them all at me. The three orbs raced at me from three different directions. I felt one swerve over to my right, the other slid to the left, and the last one rose above my head height.

They were moving fast and I had no time to react.

Don't react, anticipate.

The orb on my right, angled downward before shooting straight at me. The orb on my left started moving erratically in some impossible oscillating pattern, where it would go up and down, but still steadily headed for me. The last orb skimmed the ceiling in a straight line, but blazed a trail for my head.

I let my senses expand further, focused on the erratic orb and extended a hand, blasting a wide arc of flame in its direction. It weaved above and then below, avoiding the blast completely.

I dodged to the side and let the right orb sail past me, while the orb near the ceiling clipped me in a shoulder, throwing me off balance as the last orb slammed into my stomach as I missed it with Ebonsoul.

I doubled over in pain as the last orb disappeared.

"Impressive," Monty said. "That was well done."

"Well...done?" I said between gasps. "Which part exactly was well done? My horrible imitation of a punching bag as your orbs tenderized me, or the part where I blocked that last orb with my stomach?"

"All of it," he said with a nod. "I didn't expect you to avoid any of them."

"What?" I asked. "You didn't expect—?"

"The key was that you were able to sense them coming with your eyes closed," he said. "That was the purpose of this exercise. Now, again. Get ready."

"What? No."

"Yes," he said, forming more dangerous-looking orbs. "We continue until you can't continue any longer."

"This is abuse."

"This is a much kinder version than what I had to undergo," he said. "Consider yourself fortunate."

"I'm not feeling very fortunate at the moment."

"This was never about your feelings," he said. "Let those go."

He released another swarm.

I didn't do so well this time or the several times after that. After I lost count of the swarms, and Ebonsoul felt like it weighed fifty pounds, he announced we were almost done—one more swarm.

I was thankful since my vision had started to blur and double. On the last orb attack, Monty must've realized I was running out of steam.

As the orbs closed on me, I saw Ebonsoul vanish from my hand. I tried to form my darkflame, but only managed a dark sputter as the flames formed for a split second and immediately vanished.

The first orb impacted my face, spinning me around; I lost my balance and was gracefully introduced to the not-so-soft stone floor. I didn't even register if the rest of the swarm impacted my body. The last thing I remembered as I lost consciousness was the cool, stone floor against my face.

I opened my eyes to the harsh lighting of the infirmary. I was in the process of getting a thorough tongue-lashing from my overly eager hellhound.

He had both forepaws on the edge of the bed and was proceeding to administer his version of first aid. If he kept it up, I was going to need first aid from his first aid.

It wasn't the overabundance of saliva threatening to drown me that brought me back to consciousness, but the stench that was escaping my hellhound's mouth. My burning eyes started to water, and it became difficult to breathe as he applied his tongue therapy to every inch of my face.

"What is that horrible smell?" I asked, nearly gagging. "Did something die in here?"

My hellhound was hovering over me.

He was usually walking next to me. Seeing him from this perspective, I could understand why he would be menacing. He was actually getting quite large. The fact that he was mostly muscle was intimidating.

I noticed the runes along his flanks were glowing softly.

There were new symbols I hadn't noticed before—strange.

He shifted positions, threatening to tip the bed over.

<Stop that, you're going to tip the bed over.>

<I won't. I'm healing you, bondmate.>

<Healing me from what? I don't need healing.>

<The angry man said you were hurt. I'm healing you from your injuries. If you ate more meat, you wouldn't get hurt so often. Then one day you could be mighty.>

<Ugh! I don't need healing! You can stop trying to drown me!>

<The angry man said to make sure I used extra saliva. He said he would give me extra meat if I used extra saliva. That my mighty saliva would heal you and make you stronger.>

I glared at Monty as I tried to avoid the tongue attack.

"Mighty saliva, really?" I said, looking at Monty. "You promised him extra meat for extra saliva?"

"I needed to make sure that any injury you suffered would be healed by the extraordinary curative properties of your hellhound's saliva," he said with a straight face. "I knew it would mitigate whatever damage you may have suffered during your recent training session. No precaution can be too great and no expense was spared."

"Expense spared, what expense?"

"Do you realize I had to procure a sizable amount of meat from Ezra's?"

"We get the pastrami for free," I deadpanned. "What expense?"

"It's the principle that matters," he said. "I made sure to get him prime pastrami from Ezra's. That is no small feat."

"This beefy blackmail is a little much," I said. "You do realize I heal?"

"As I said, no precaution can be too great," he repeated. "I would hate for you to have lasting effects from all those orb impacts."

"Hilarious," I said, trying to shove my hellhound away. "The mage humor is killing me. I will remember this." I focused on Peaches, and really moved him off the bed. It took some major effort. "Okay, boy, enough trying to drown me. Monty, think I could get a towel? A little help?"

Monty handed me a towel as I heard giggles next to me, the source being just out of sight.

Young girlish giggles.

I figured these two were the reason my hellhound's breath had become weaponized. They were becoming dangerous. It was only a matter of time before they started devising seriously threatening schemes.

"You two turned his breath into something lethal," I said, glancing at the two young girls holding in the laughter behind me. "What did you do? His breath has never smelled that bad."

"We fed him pastrami with red onions and garlic," Cece said. "He ate it all up!"

"He really liked it, but it made his breath really smell bad, so we saved the smell for you," Peanut volunteered. "Aunt Mo said she made the red onions and garlic extra strong because he's a hellhound and he needs *really* strong food."

"She is actually trying to kill me," I mumbled to myself. "She seasoned the pastrami?"

"Uncle Tristan gave her the meat," Peanut said, glancing at Monty. "And she said she needed to prepare it for Peaches."

"So this was a team hit job," I said, looking at them and feigning seriousness. "You all were in on it."

"Only Uncle Dex didn't want to," Cece added. "He said we were being cruel and unusual."

"What you've created is an especially deadly form of hellitosis," I said, still pushing my hellhound away. "Agh! Stay back!"

Peaches came closer and slapped me across the face again with his tongue of doom. The breath punched me in the nose and then choked me around the neck, the smell refusing to let go of my lungs.

"We need to create hellhound mints, anything that can defeat this extra strength hellitosis," I said. "Wow! That's bad. That breath can be a weapon all by itself!"

I wiped my face down as the girls laughed again, running out of the room with my hellhound in tow. He chuffed and rumbled as he chased them.

"They're actually good for each other," I said, watching them run out of the room. "I've never seen him take to anyone like that." I looked around. "Where's Rags?"

"With the Morrigan."

"The Morrigan?" I asked, concerned. "Why would she be with the Morrigan?"

"She is undergoing a specific training," Monty said. "Cece's examination is fast approaching. Ragnarok must be ready to assist her through her testing."

"She gets tested too?"

"Yes, as her Guardian, she must prove herself capable of protecting Cece from every possible threat they may encounter," Monty said, his voice grim. "Failure is not an option."

"That sounds a little final," I said, glancing at him. "What happens if she fails?"

"Who? Cecelia or her Guardian?"

"Either or both?"

"Cecelia is testing for a position of power within the hierarchy of her family—Jotnar ice mages," Monty explained. "Their norms and customs are vastly different from what we are accustomed to."

"That's a long explanation to not tell me what happens if she fails."

"Cecelia and her Guardian are very similar to you and your creature," Monty said. "As Cecelia grows in power so does her Guardian."

"Still haven't explained what happens if she fails," I said. "Why are you beating around the bush?"

"Because I know you. Even more, I know how protective you are around children," he said. "You will undoubtedly misconstrue the consequences of failure and do something we will all regret."

"How do you know I will misconstrue anything?" I countered as I sat up. "I don't even know what the consequences are yet."

"Simon, you rushed into a warehouse inhabited by Rakshasa after being contracted by a god," he said. "This was after being informed that your client was a god, and that the person he had hired you to intercept was a goddess."

"I had no proof of their divinity."

"I would think the Rakshasa patrolling the warehouse would be a fairly clear indicator of the otherworldly nature of your client and his target."

"I'm not seeing the point here."

"Why did you take that case?" he asked, reminding me of

my recent conversation with Kali. "Honestly, what spurred you to take it on? Don't say Ramirez. I know he's your friend, but you were on board before he got into the details. I was still surveying the plans of the warehouse, and you were ready to rush in sight unseen. Tell me why."

"You know why," I said. "It's crystal clear."

"The children," he said, and I looked away as I nodded. "You wanted to save the children."

"And we did," I said. "I would do it all again, if I had to."

"I know," he said. "That is why I'm hesitant to share the details about Cecelia's testing."

"Monty," I said, feeling the anger rise in my chest. "I think right about now you should share the details with me."

"Take a breath and calm down," he said. "There's no justification for anger, at least not yet. Besides, as her primary tutor or tutors, we have a measure of recourse available to us. We have a voice."

"Monty..."

He held up a hand in surrender.

"If Cecelia fails, she will be exiled from the Jotnar, and Ragnarok, her guardian, will be put down," he said, his voice somber. "Some of her family may even request she be erased before she is exiled."

"Erased and exiled?" I asked, having a difficult time keeping my rage in check. "Does she know this?"

"She's a child," Monty said, looking out of the doorway where Cece had run out into the corridor minutes earlier. "How do I explain this to her? That her own family will cast her out, while some may want her stripped of her power?"

"Can we attend her testing?"

"Simon, I know what you are thinking," he said, giving me a hard look. "We are not Jotnar. If we interfere in her testing, we may jeopardize her standing within the Jotnar community."

"Can we attend her testing? Yes or no?"

"Yes," he said with a sigh. "As her instructors, we are obligated to be at her testing since we have directly influenced her acquisition of skill and expertise in regards to her ability."

"Good," I said. "I give you my word. I will not interfere."

He sighed and nodded.

"That is the proper and right course of action," he said. "We don't want to start a war with—"

"I wasn't finished," I said, cutting him off. "As long as they don't try and erase her, I will keep out of it. If they try and strip her of her power, they're going to have to deal with me. I can promise you, that is not going to end well...for them."

"We have to handle this differently," Monty said. "There are methods and protocols we must observe. Overt violence will solve nothing."

"Cece is not being erased," I said. "They want to exile her? Fine, I will stay out of it. She always has a place to stay, either with us, or here at the school. That's going to hurt, but she'll grow past the pain."

"You don't understand—"

"Let me finish, then you can educate me on the rituals and procedures that must be followed," I said. "Erasure is stealing something from her, something that makes her who she is. I can't believe you would let them erase her."

"I never said I would *allow* that option," he said, his voice hard. "I said there are other options."

"Like?" I asked. "Because right now, it looks like she either gets erased, or we go to war with the Jotnar. I can guarantee you option one is not happening. I'm kind of open for option two."

"If she fails her examination and they present erasure as an option, I will introduce my uncle and the Morrigan as surrogates," he said. "Sadly, we cannot countermand a recommendation of exile, but we can intervene in the case of erasure, via surrogates."

"Surrogate what?"

"Guardians."

"You can do that?"

"There are clauses and provisos that allow me to pursue that course of action, provided you don't blast the Jotnar into oblivion and spark a mage war."

"Why didn't you start with that?"

"You were already in a war with the ice mages, before I had a chance to explain the details."

"What about Rags?" I said. "Can we save her too?"

"Same clause that takes custodianship of Cecelia would include Ragnarok," Monty assured me. "I've discussed this with my uncle and the Morrigan. They are both in accord. They had planned on taking this step with Peanut; extending the invitation to Cecelia is a delicate matter, due to her position in the Jotnar and the upcoming examination."

"She may want to just be here with Dex and the Morrigan," I said, looking down the corridor. "Especially if she gets to have Peanut for a sister."

"My thoughts exactly," he said. "That being said, we will train her to pass her examination before sharing any of this with her. She should be free to make her choice, free of any pressure."

"Won't they force her into the Jotnar hierarchy if she passes?"

"She has a choice," Monty said. "Only if she passes."

"Then we better make sure she passes."

"One thing at a time," he said. "We have a Grand Council to deal with, which means we need to find—"

"The Spartan."

He nodded as the Morrigan appeared in the room.

EIGHT

My heart attempted to jump out of my chest and run down the corridor as the Morrigan materialized next to my bed.

"I hear you had an illuminating conversation with your goddess?" she said. "That will facilitate things...in the future."

"You nearly gave me a heart attack, appearing like that," I said. "Are you trying to kill me?"

She wore a black on black ensemble of...I want to say it was a dress, but it was closer to a shroud of darkness that appeared to be a long, form-fitting dress. Her hair hung loose, and almost seemed to melt into the shroud of energy that surrounded her.

Her eyes flared slightly with green energy as she looked from Monty to me. All around her, I could pick up the scent of fear. Not *her* fear—I doubted she feared anything in existence—rather it was a scent that generated fear.

It was an irrational, mind-crushing fear, trying to blot out everything else from my mind. I started sweating, and I could feel my heart rate increase. At the same time, a chill came over me as my breath came in short gasps.

I was about to say something to Monty, but all the saliva

in my mouth had disappeared and it felt like I had swallowed a cup of sand. I looked to the sides, searching for the closest exit.

What is going on?

As she stood there, thoughts of running out of the infirmary filled my mind. In fact, getting as far from her as possible was the only thing I could focus on. She must have noticed my reaction. I didn't see Monty melting down or Peaches having a reaction, so I figured she was unleashing some custom-made terror just for me.

"My apologies," she said with a slight nod. "Let me dispel that fear."

With a gesture from her, the fear was gone.

"You were saying?" she continued. "Can you speak?"

I nodded and swallowed hard, looking for the words as my brain restarted. Her fear effect had left my body ragged. My legs felt like I had just done back-to-back marathons; the rest of me was worn out from a major dump of adrenaline.

There was no fight, flight or freeze response to what she had just done—it was all flight, period.

How could anyone even stand against that kind of power?

The answer was simple.

They couldn't.

"I...I was asking if you were trying to kill me?" I repeated, realizing how foolish the question was. I nearly melted into a gibbering puddle just standing next to her. How much harder would it be to end me? "What was that fear?"

She smiled.

"Why would I *try* to kill you?" she asked, looking at me. "If I wanted you dead, I would simply end your life. It would be bothersome, since you wouldn't *remain* dead."

"My curse."

She nodded.

"Then your goddess would want to have words about your

demise," she said. "She is quite attached to her Marked, not that she would ever admit it."

"Attached?"

I know, I have an amazing skill with words.

In my defense, my brain was just getting back online. The terror that had gripped me seconds earlier had shut down everything in my head. I was actually surprised my brain was still working and forming words. I should have been curled up into a ball on the ground, in a pool of terror-induced drool.

"Yes, attached," the Morrigan said. "Truly, I don't know why. Suffering leads to growth. She is actually concerned for your well-being."

"She has a funny way of showing it," I said, reflexively rubbing my forehead. "Her mark hasn't done me any favors or won me any friends. Not to mention the whole successor thing. If *that* is her way of being attached, I would hate to see if she didn't care."

The Morrigan gave me a look that froze my blood.

"You would *not* want to be on her bad side, Simon, trust me."

I held up a hand in surrender.

"I'm just saying she has a funny way of showing she cares."

"True, she is Kali the Destroyer," she said. "What did you expect? You interfered with her plan. You chose to confront her. You chose to risk your life for those children."

"I know she made it extremely clear when we spoke."

"Perhaps this will make it easier to understand," she said. "The day you chose to stand against her, you died. You forfeited your life; she just hasn't collected it...yet."

"She said something similar to that," I said. "My life is hers."

She nodded.

"Your curse comes with a *cost*. *All* power carries a cost.

Spoken or not, it exists and *must* be paid. There are no exceptions; remember that."

"I will," I said and nodded, still wary. "Gives new meaning to living on borrowed time."

"Apt, still," she said, giving me a pensive look I didn't appreciate—it was one of those 'what else could I test on this lab rat?' kind of looks. "However, now that you mention it, we've never really tested the outer limits of your curse. How *dead* do you need to be to *stay* dead?"

"Can't you just ask Kali and she can tell you?" I offered. "Some of these things are better left off as theory, don't you think?"

"I *am* intrigued," she said. "But that will have to wait for another time. Perhaps I'll discuss it with your goddess. It's purely for academic reasons."

"No, thank you," I said. "There's really no reason to test the outer limits of my curse, thank you."

"Hmm, I would think you'd *want* to know how far you could push yourself, before it became fatal," she said. "Consider it. It's good information to have if you're going to use your new name."

"My *new* name?"

"Deathless?" she said, looking from me to Monty. "I thought this was your new accepted name."

"I didn't get the memo," I said. "What's wrong with Simon? I like Simon. Simon is a good name, it doesn't immediately trigger beings into trying to disintegrate me."

"Nothing, except Deathless has an air of menace Simon lacks, don't you think?" she asked. "I prefer Deathless, but it is *your* name."

"I think I'll stick with Simon," I said. "If I change my name to Deathless, it's an invitation. All my enemies will want to find out if it's true. 'Is he really deathless? Let's find out just how deathless he really is.'"

"Which is why I suggested testing the outer limits of your curse," she said. "That information is instrumental in your facing those who would want to test your new name."

"I'm not changing my name."

"Names have power," she said in almost a whisper. "Consider my names. I am the Phantom Queen, the Great Queen, I have gone by Macha, Badb, and Nemain. I have countless others given to me over time. Some know me as the Nightmare Queen, while others have called me the Chooser of the Slain."

"I don't want to change my name."

"None of the many names I am known by is my true name," she continued. "The power of names is derived from the transformation they create."

"I don't understand."

"All of my names define aspects of what I am, not who I am," she said. "The distinction is subtle but important."

"Deathless is what I am, not who I am?" I said. "Sounds like the same thing."

"It's not, but you will discover that soon enough."

"I still prefer Simon," I said. "It feels safer."

She laughed.

"One thing your life is not, is safe," she said. "Names have a way of sneaking up on you. Once one person calls you Deathless, it starts to spread. Before you know it, enemies are calling you Deathless."

"That's exactly what I'm trying to avoid."

"Sooner rather than later, you'll have that one enemy that wants to test if your name is real or just bravado. Then it's death threats twenty-four hours a day. It can become quite tiring, truly."

I just stared at her before composing myself.

"Did you need us for something?" Monty asked, thankfully changing the subject. "Does my uncle need something?"

"He is busy at the moment, interviewing one of our new instructors for the school," she said, looking off to the side. "I came to inform you of a new development."

"A new development?" I asked. "That doesn't sound good."

"Good is a relative term," she said. "Speaking of enemies, the Grand Council has delegated your apprehension and subsequent extermination to a new emissary, Emissary Salya Amrita."

"Emissary Salya?" Monty said, incredulous. "Are they mad?"

"I have to admit, I am somewhat impressed," she said. "Having Emissary Salya as your enemy is no light matter. I'm sure Kali will be quite pleased."

"This is not good." I said. "I'm not exactly focused on making Kali happy by having the most deadly of enemies after me."

"You may want to reconsider your focus."

"The Grand Council is acting directly against us now?" Monty asked. "This reaction has nothing to do with my uncle and the removal of the Golden Circle?"

"I'm certain that plays into this, but you two, well three," —she glanced at my hellhound, who had materialized quietly under my bed with a soft rumble— "including your astounding hound, killed an Emissary and a Magistrate," she answered. "Did you think that would go unanswered? This is the Grand Council. They have eradicated entire sects for *perceived* slights. You openly defied them...and won. In their minds, an example must be made."

"Wouldn't it be better to make an example of a living being?" I asked. "If they kill us they won't be able to make much of an example."

"I agree," the Morrigan said. "Normally, I would say they want you dead or alive, but I believe we are past such niceties.

Since they tasked her, it would seem the Grand Council would prefer you both dead."

"Bloody hell, they really enlisted the Immortal Spear?" Monty said, and I heard real fear in his voice. "How long?"

"Immortal Spear?" I asked. "What does that mean?"

"It's never quite long enough, is it?" the Morrigan said, ignoring me. "I would say a sense of urgency is required on your part. You can't remain here much longer. I suggest you find the Hidden Hand. At least before Salya does."

"Wait, what?" I asked, confused. "Why would she be looking for the Hidden Hand?"

"I thought the answer would be apparent," she said.

"No, not really," I said. "The answer is not apparent. Not even remotely apparent." I looked over at Monty who shook his head. "No, the answer is not apparent to either of us."

"What is it that you need to do, Simon?"

"Context?"

"Staying alive and keeping those around you alive," she said with a small smile. "Is that enough context?"

"That's plenty of context," I said, feeling some of the fear returning. "I need to get stronger, specifically my shield."

"How many times have you used your dawnward?"

I looked at her, surprised.

"How did you—?"

"It's not a secret, *Aspis*," she said. "Now, has it become apparent?"

"No," I said. "It hasn't."

"Yes," Monty said. "It makes perfect sense."

She turned to me.

"Kali would not have chosen you if you were too stupid to survive," she said, poking my chest with a finger. "This means that she believes you are intelligent enough to figure out this new world you live in. The new world you are part of. It is time you get past the awe and wonder, and accept that this is your life now." She poked me in the forehead. "Now, use that brain of yours and figure it out."

She stepped back, crossed her arms, and stared at me.

"What, now?" I asked, looking at her. "You want me to figure out why Emissary Salsa is going after the Hidden Hand based on how many times I've used my dawnward? That's impossible."

"That response sounds like you need *incentive*."

The way she said that last word meant pain and agony. What was it with these death goddesses and the pain?

"No incentive required," I said, raising a hand. "Give me a second—not a literal second. Hold on."

"If the Grand Council is sending the Emissary after the Hidden Hand, based on my use of a dawnward, it means they've been watching me."

She nodded.

"They study their enemies and *potential* enemies," she said. "It's how they have remained in power for so long."

"It means they know about Monty and my bonds to this new world I find myself in," I said, searching her impassive face which gave nothing away. "It means they know about my dawnward and my training, or lack thereof."

"Their assessment of you, while thorough, appears to be flawed," she answered. "Why do I say this?"

"Because we're alive and Alain and Emeric aren't."

"Correct," she said with a nod. "They underestimated you and lost a Magistrate and one of their valued Emissaries. They won't make that mistake again."

"I'm supposing a heartfelt apology won't work?"

"No, stop stalling and continue," she said. "Why Emissary Salya?"

"If she's as fearsome as she sounds, it's part of their not making the same mistake twice," I said. "This time they're going for the overkill method. Send the strongest they have."

"Yes, one of the stronger Emissaries, but not the strongest," she said. "They don't respect you that much, not yet. Hopefully you will change their mind."

"And if we don't?"

"You will be dead," she answered. "Salya Amrita, The Immortal Spear, is virtually unkillable. She wields the Iron Spear, a weapon of immense power. Rumor has it, it was runed by Murugan himself, but that rumor has never been proven. Most likely it was some Archmage among the Grand Council who runed her weapon."

"Her weapon was runed by an Archmage?" I asked in disbelief. "We're supposed to go up against that?"

"Yes; she is also an accomplished mage in her own right, without the weapon."

"You're really not selling this."

"I'm not selling anything," the Morrigan said. "You will face her, it is inevitable. Now tell me why."

"If the Grand Council knows about my dawnward and its weakness, they have to know I will try to make it stronger," I said, seeing the pieces fall into place. "They have to know I would look for someone who could help me and my shield get stronger as the Aspis."

"They know all the beings of power in your immediate circle," she said. "None of us can help you with your dawnward."

"Can't or won't?"

"Can't," she said with a slight air of menace. "Which leaves?"

"The Spartan or Hidden Hand, whom I'm assuming are one and the same?"

"Yes," she said. "Why him?"

"That, I don't know," I said. "It makes no sense. There have to be plenty of people with the knowledge to increase my shield power."

"Yes, in fact there are, but remember, I said names have power," she replied. "You are designated as the *Aspis*. There is only *one* living Aspis at a time, which means—?"

"The number of people I can turn to for training is limited too," I answered, as it finally made sense. "If I'm going to increase my ability as the Aspis, I need to see the Spartan."

"They are being proactive," Monty said. "The Grand Council doesn't necessarily know he is going to see the Spartan, but they know that eventually he must, if he is to increase his ability as an Aspis."

"Precisely."

"They are removing my options for getting stronger," I said. "Makes it easier to take me and those near me out if I can't make a stronger shield. Kill the shieldbearer and everyone is exposed."

"I would say so," she said. "As it stands, your dawnward is weak, but one of its operating principles is that it taps into—?"

"Life-force," I said, dropping the final piece into place. "It uses my life-force. The Spartan knows how to train me to use my life-force as a source of energy?"

"In this specific realm of knowledge, I would say he is the best equipped to do so," she said. "He is impossibly old and has managed to reach his age by mastery of his life-force. Even divine beings give him a wide berth, wondering if he is immortal."

"They don't know?"

"His origins are shrouded in time," she said. "He was ancient when he stood with the Spartans against the Persian Empire. Some say he is Phanes, but I can assure you he is not. Those who have met him have confirmed he is human, a very powerful and ancient human, but still a human, nevertheless."

"Who exactly is Phanes?"

"You need to study more," she said. "Let's see, in your history the Hidden Hand is rumored to be the original Deathless, Enoch, who later had his name changed to Metatron."

"The angel of life?" Monty asked. "That Metatron?"

She gave Monty a look and shook her head.

"He is *not* the angel of life," she said. "The Hidden Hand is merely an ancient mage who has managed to manipulate his life-force to such an extent that he appears to be immortal, but he is not the angel of life, nor is he Phanes, the god of life."

"He also has excellent P.R.," I said. "If he has people believing he is immortal, but it's not true, he is an excellent storyteller."

"Which is why the Grand Council is trying to remove him," Monty said. "They know the rumors are false."

She nodded.

"Hold on, are you saying there's an actual angel of life?" I asked. "Walking around? For real?"

"Why do you find that surprising?" she asked. "You frequent a delicatessen being run by Azrael, or Ezra as you call him. Why would the existence of his opposite be so hard to comprehend?"

"I just didn't...I mean, Death is—you know, Death is everywhere," I said, trying to explain the unexplainable. "An angel of life seems a little far-fetched."

"That is the effect of your modern society," she said. "Death has enjoyed a certain level of acceptance. I can assure you, Metatron exists, though I doubt he is *walking about* or running a delicatessen downtown. I do wonder about Azrael sometimes."

"So we need to find the Hidden Hand before the Emissary does," I said. "Because that's one of the only ways I can get my shield stronger."

"More than that, he can help you shape your life-force, your *extensive* life-force into a source of power that you can weaponize."

"Can't Kali or any other god do that?"

"No," she replied. "Though she cursed you alive, she cannot teach you how to use the excess life-force you now possess as a weapon. That requires a specialized knowledge that few have."

"But...but she's a goddess," I said. "How could she not know?"

"You still have so much to learn," she said. "Kali is not omniscient, nor am I. Our knowledge is vast, but only because we have existed for so long. It is not infinite, nor all-encompassing."

She handed me an envelope.

"What's this?" I asked, looking down at the envelope before opening it. "Some special message?"

"My knowledge is not all-encompassing, but I do have some excellent contacts, as does the Grand Council, partly for the same reason. They are an ancient order," she said, pointing at the envelope. "That is where you begin your search for the Hidden Hand. I would waste no time getting started."

She disappeared a second later.

NINE

I opened the envelope.

The paper was thick and cream-colored. It reminded me of parchment, though the edges were frayed. The writing, which was a deep red, was a fluid script that I couldn't decipher when I first tried to read it.

I realized after a few seconds that it was runic script.

I showed the paper to Monty and he raised an eyebrow as he took it from my hands. He turned it over a few times and examined the writing closely before shaking his head.

"Runic script?" he said, looking at the paper one more time before handing it back to me. "What does it say?"

"What do you mean, what does it say?" I asked, irritated. "It's runic script; you read runic script. That's a mage specialty, and there's only one mage standing here right now."

"I'm aware," he said, dusting off a sleeve. "That doesn't automatically grant me the ability to read *that* particular script."

"I thought all mages could read runic language?"

"Runic alphabets are a *written* form of communication, not a language," he explained. "In general, they are ancient and commonly used by mages to communicate components in specific casts, operating as ideographs to convey desired concepts."

"Is that why they're used in circles?"

"Among other items of power," he added. "Knowing a certain alphabet doesn't infer that I know them *all*. There are variations, and some mages deliberately obfuscated the meaning of some of the symbols when they used them."

"But this letter isn't that," I said, looking at the paper in my hand. "You can't read this runic script, can you?"

He shook his head as he glanced at the paper again.

"It would appear the Morrigan, along with the other people in your life, is beginning to treat you like the being of power that you are," he said. "You may not be a mage, but it doesn't mean you lack resources or abilities. It's time you accepted that truth. Those runes are coded for you, and you only."

"What does that mean?"

"It means only *you* can read them," he said, pointing at the paper. "She probably expected you to ask me, and eliminated that possibility from the equation by taking this step. It's quite extraordinary when you think about it."

"Eliminated the possibility from the equation?" I asked, holding up the paper. "How am I supposed to read this? I don't read runes."

"The same way you read the runes in the lab, I suppose," he said. "If you're having difficulty, I could supply some life-threatening orbs to give you required additional motivation."

I stared at him.

"Mage humor, really," I deadpanned. "Not funny, not even a little."

"I thought it was a *little* funny," he said with a slight smile, before becoming serious. "You need to focus and use your innersight. If you could read the runes in the lab, albeit under stress, you can read these. Coded runes work by channeling power through the item containing them. In this case, you channel energy through the paper."

He pointed at the paper again.

"Focus," he continued with a nod. "Channel power through the paper and read the runes. It's that simple and that complicated."

"How long did it take you to learn to read runes?"

"Once I was comfortable using my ability, close to five or six years," he said. "The hardest part was comprehending the concept of energy manipulation."

"It took you five or six years, and I'm supposed to just *know* this?" I asked, incredulous. "How old were you?"

"You misunderstand," he answered. "I *was* five or six when I first began reading runes. It's the most rudimentary of all skills, one you should have mastered when you learned your magic missile. What do you call it?" He snapped his fingers. "It's like learning your ABC's."

"Oh," I said, embarrassed. "I didn't realize it was that easy."

"It's not, and I was advanced. However"—he motioned to the paper in my hand—"you've proven you can read runes," he said, reassuring me. "Now you merely have to apply yourself. You can do it." He waved me on. "Go on, you heard her, we don't have the luxury of time. We need to find the Hidden Hand before Salya does. You're holding the first clue to his location in your hand."

I looked down at the paper.

"Why couldn't she have just told us?" I protested. "That would've made our lives much easier."

"I don't think the Morrigan, of all people, is overly concerned about making our lives easier," he said. "Why didn't Kali just increase the strength of your shield while you were there, or bestow some of her vast knowledge upon you as her Marked One? I'm certain that would have been within the scope of her power."

"Because making my life easier wouldn't be as entertaining?"

He narrowed his eyes at me and slowly shook his head.

"Do not make the mistake of hubris," he said. "Yes, they pay an inordinate amount of attention to your actions, but do not, for one moment, presume that you are the center of their attention. They are gods. On the list of what they focus on, *you* are extremely low on the list, if you are on it at all."

"Well, now my spirits are uplifted."

"Glad I could be of service. Do stop stalling, help is not coming. I thought you'd realize that by now. We hold our destiny in our hands."

I nodded as I focused on the paper in my hands.

"Funny you would mention it," I said. "She actually addressed that, when I was at the temple."

"What did she say?"

"She said: *The Marked of Kali must learn to tap into the power of the mark he or she bears. Without any assistance from me. To assist you would negate the purpose of the mark.* That's pretty much verbatim. Everything I need from her is in her mark, I just have to tap into it."

"She didn't happen to instruct you on how to do *that*, did she?"

"You know, somehow she left out the mark tapping instructions in our conversation," I said. "Or maybe she did share them, but I was so busy being bounced around the temple grounds that I had a hard time paying attention and missed them. What do *you* think?"

"I didn't think she would, but it doesn't hurt to ask."

"Actually it does," I said, thinking back to my recent conversation with Kali. "With Kali, it could be fatal. She's a strong believer in the whole 'an image is worth a thousand words' school of thought."

My hellhound rumbled by my feet and looked up at me. We were facing stronger enemies, stronger than us. The people in our lives who wanted to help us couldn't, without escalating everything to unacceptable levels.

Actually, by not helping us, they *were* helping us—to get stronger.

I had to stop thinking that all of this was unfair. No one ever said life was fair. I was being immature expecting it to be fair.

I had made the choice.

I accepted the case and I chose to go to the warehouse that night. I was walking this path because I chose to step on it. No one else was responsible.

It all started and ended with me.

I held the paper in front of me and focused. I let the power flow through my body and into my hands. The runic script on the paper began to shift and transform, forming different symbols, symbols that slowly became legible to me.

"The script is changing," I said, still focused on the paper. "I can make it out."

"What does it say?" Monty asked. "Where do we need to go?"

"It says: *Beneath the temple of Athena, when Selene's chariot is at its height, the doorway to the undying mage's domain will appear. To gain entrance, you must walk with Hades, but he must not have sway over you. With Charon's obol, all doors will open to you—choose wisely. Those who cling to life, die. Those who cling to death, live.*"

"I guess expecting an actual map to his location is a step too far?" I asked, turning the page over to see if there was any more, but those were the only words on the paper. "I'm not expecting a Rand McNally masterpiece, but is an address too much to ask? Maybe some lines with an X to mark where this door is?"

"Memorize it," Monty said, pointing at the words. "Do it, now."

I looked at the words and committed them to memory. It was much easier than I expected.

"I don't know why you want me to mem—" I started as the runic symbols began to shift again. "What's going on?"

"Once the message is deciphered, aside from it being keyed to you, it codes itself again, this time ensuring no one else can read it. Not even you could decipher that message now, despite the fact that it was meant for you."

"Is this thing going to go all Mission Impossible on me?" I asked, holding the paper at arm's length. "Is it going to explode?"

"Don't be so dramatic," he said. "It's a one-time effect. The only thing that's impossible would be trying to decipher that script."

I focused, letting energy flow into the paper again, and nothing happened. The energy flowed and I just looked at the paper. After a few seconds, it suddenly disintegrated into dust.

"What the—?" I said, stepping back from the mini-dust cloud that had suddenly formed in front of me. "It really is a one-time thing."

"You tried to decipher it again, didn't you?" Monty asked, looking at the dust. "I told you it wouldn't work. Did you commit it to memory?"

"Yes, though I don't entirely understand most of it."

"Recite it again," Monty said. "Slowly, please, there are some parts I need to process."

"You understood what it meant?"

"Some of it, yes," he said with a short nod. "Other parts are obscure."

"Other parts are obscure?" I asked. "Which? Like everything after beneath the temple?"

"Recite it again, please."

"Sure, it said: *Beneath the temple of Athena, when Selene's chariot is at its height, the doorway to the undying mage's domain will appear. To gain entrance, you must walk with Hades, but he must not have sway over you. With Charon's obol, all doors will open to you—choose wisely. Those who cling to life, die. Those who cling to death, live.*"

"There is much to decipher there," Monty said, rubbing his chin. "Most of it is contextual. We will need access to the Library. Are you ready to move?"

I nodded.

"Move *where* exactly?" I asked. "I don't think the Montague School of Battlemagic has a library yet. Does it?"

"The school has always had access to the Library," Monty said, and then looked me over. "It may be a good idea to change your clothes first. You look like you've been rolling in the dirt with an angry ogre for the last few hours, and lost."

I looked down at my clothes and winced.

"You'd think Kali would repair my clothing after she tossed me all over the temple," I said. "Hey, do you think I could learn a clothing repair cast?"

"If your sausage cast is any indicator of your casting ability, it may be easier to get a change of clothing and physically change," he said, shaking his head and pointing to the closet. "I'd also argue it's safer. The last thing you need is to have your clothes come apart at the seams while someone or something is trying to end you. That would be the height of embarrassment and a quick way to die."

"You know, you could just say, no, you can't learn that cast," I said, heading over to the nearby closet for a change of clothing. "No need to bring up my lack of sausage-making skills."

"Actually, with enough practice, you could probably fashion a few simple items of clothing," he suggested. "If you really devoted some study to it, you could, despite your inherent lack of casting ability, create a fairly durable sheet. That would work quite well on cold nights to keep you warm."

"A sheet?" I glared at him. "If I practice, I could cast a sheet? You mean a bedsheet?"

"Do you know of another kind of sheet?" he asked. "Yes, a fairly durable bedsheet."

"Seriously?"

"It would be top-notch, if you practice enough," he deadpanned. "Never underestimate the utility of a well-made sheet, though I have heard a good towel always comes in handy. Especially if you're prone to panic.

"I don't panic."

"Just a suggestion," he added. "Towels do have more utility."

"I'm going to pass on the sheet and towel practice, thanks," I snapped. "I'll just change into this set of clothes here, if you don't mind."

"I don't mind at all, in fact I'd prefer it if you did," he said. "I'll meet you outside, once you're ready."

"Where exactly is this library we're going to, anyway?" I asked as he headed for the door. "I don't recall Dex or the Morrigan mentioning a new library."

"That's because it's not new," he said. "Meet me outside and I'll explain. Do not dally."

He stepped outside, leaving me alone with my thoughts and my hellhound. I looked down at Peaches and placed the new set of clothes on the bed.

It was a black T-shirt and dark jeans ensemble, complete with a jacket. I focused my innersight and runes exploded in my vision.

That was new.

Each item of clothing was covered in softly glowing violet and red runes. I could make out most of them, which was new for me. I realized they were mostly designed for protection and the durability of the item itself. Some of the runes were to increase the resilience against casting, while others were to enhance the clothing against physical damage.

I would have to take more time to study runes from now on. I had a feeling this information would come in handy. I couldn't afford to be walking around with powerful enemies and ignorant about something that could protect or harm me.

Those days were over.

I started changing my clothes.

"Criticizing my Healthy Hellhound Delight," I grumbled as I changed and glanced down at my hellhound. "That is probably the best sausage ever created; he just doesn't know sausage. Right, boy?"

<Your sausage is the best sausage—for breaking stomachs.>

Everyone was a critic.

I finished changing and stepped outside with my hellhound in tow.

TEN

Monty was standing outside of the infirmary.

Dex had arrived and was having some words with him as I approached. Dex nodded at me as I stepped close.

"Ach, boy, I heard about the Immortal Spear," he said, shaking his head. "You need to find H as quickly as you can. Salya is no Alain. She will try to make short work of ye. Do you understand?"

"I do," I said. "I just didn't understand the message the Morrigan gave me."

"You will," Dex said with a nod. "I've given my nephew access to the Library. You'll be able to start your journey from there."

I looked around the grounds.

There were plenty of new buildings. In fact, the school campus was growing at an incredible rate. It could easily rival any of the largest universities I knew.

It wasn't hard to imagine that one of the new buildings could be a library—actually that made the most sense. A School for Battlemagic would need an extensive library to help the students learn about the casts. Not to mention it would need a massive research wing. The buildings weren't named, so I couldn't tell if one of them was designated as the new library.

"Thanks," I said, looking around at the buildings near us. "Just point us in the right direction and we'll get started."

"Aye, Main Building, lower level," he said. "We have access to the new branch through a connection there. Last door to your right. It's runed with the name; should be easy for you, now. Mind the circles."

"The circles?" I asked warily. "What circles?"

"The ones that will send you to the other side of the grounds if you're not careful," Dex said. "You'll see." He placed a hand on my shoulder. "Listen to H, he knows what he's talking about. His lessons may very well save your life."

"I will," I said. "Will you be able to help? Does Salya have a Magistrate assistant?"

"No."

I sighed in relief.

"That's good," I said. "Emeric wasn't exactly a pushover. Grand Council Magistrates are major threats. That's actually good news."

His expression became grim as he shook his head.

"Actually, boy, it's not," Dex corrected. "She doesn't have Magistrates assisting her because the Grand Council deemed her too dangerous."

"What?" I asked. "She's too dangerous to have Magistrates? What does that even mean?"

He gave me a solemn nod.

"You know how you feel around Nemain when it's being wielded?" he asked. "The fear?"

"It's a little hard to forget," I said. "You mean terrorized into mind-numbing fear with a strong desire to run away as far and as fast as possible? That feeling?"

"Despite feeling like you're about to die from the fright, it won't literally end your life," he explained. "Not unless I want it to. Her weapon is different."

"Different how?" I asked, shelving that comment about Nemain being able to kill an enemy from fright. It made sense, being a weapon belonging to the Morrigan. "What does it do?"

"Emissary Salya's weapon has a physical deadly area of effect," he said and I felt a cold pit of fear form in my stomach. "Her Immortal Spear has a, let's call it a diameter of death. Anyone caught in it—Magistrates, Sanitizers, anyone —well, let's just say they don't survive long enough to tell the tale. When she wields that weapon, it creates a moving killing field around her. That's without her actually hitting you. She is an accomplished spear practitioner."

"What the hell," I said in a barely audible voice. "So if the aura of death doesn't kill you, her attacks with the actual spear *will*?"

He nodded.

"More or less, boy," he said. "I don't have to warn you to be wary of her when you face her. You're probably one of the few that can, Deathless. I wouldn't be surprised if the Grand Council knows about your special condition."

"How does the Grand Council justify keeping her as an Emissary?" I asked. "She just goes around killing everything?"

"They limit her activities because she's so dangerous," he said. "Which means you two have become a threat worth consideration if they've unleashed her on ye."

"I'm flattered, we've attracted enough attention to get the Emissary of Death after us, great," I said, feeling my mouth go dry. "Is that why she's a solo operative?"

"Aye, Magistrates and any other field operatives have a short life expectancy around her," he said. "Very few have volunteered to assist her after what happened to her last three Magistrates. After that, the Grand Council stopped assigning Magistrates to her. It was getting too costly."

"How strong is she?" I asked. "I mean as a mage."

"You recall Alain, and the power he wielded?"

"He killed me," I said, my voice hard. "It's a little hard to forget."

"Good, hold onto that anger; you're going to need it," he answered. "She's just as strong, if not stronger than he was."

"Will you be able to help?" I asked, looking off to the side at the sprawling campus. "We weren't able to face Alain without your help."

"I wasn't the one who stopped him," he said, shaking his head and pointing at Monty and me. "That was you two and your hound. I provided a distraction."

"We might need that distraction again, if she's stronger than Alain," I said. "Do you really think the Grand Council knows about my curse?"

"I can't see another reason to unleash this particular Emissary," he said. "This is like using a hammer to kill an especially annoying ant." Then he cracked a wicked grin. "Except the ant in this case is powerful enough to destroy the hammer."

"This ant would feel much better if you could assist," I said, returning his grin with a slight smile of my own. "If only to scare the piss out of her."

He rested a hand on my shoulder and looked from Monty to me.

"I'll do all I can, but much of this rests on you lads' shoulders," he said. "I will handle what needs to be handled on my end. This isn't over with the Grand Council, but if you manage to stop Salya, you can convince them to restrain themselves or..."

"Or?"

"They'll just go in the other direction, total scorched earth and send one of the five after you two," he said, rubbing his chin in a very Montaguean way. "It's hard to tell with the Grand Council sometimes; they rarely react as expected. Things I thought would set them off, they ignore, and things I thought they would absolutely ignore"—he gestured to the school grounds with an outstretched arm—"well, here we are."

"You thought they would ignore you borrowing the Golden Circle?" I asked, incredulous. "Really?"

"They despised the Golden Circle," he said, his voice filled with a controlled menace. "They tried to destroy the sect repeatedly in its long existence. I thought I was doing them a favor, removing it from under their influence."

"They didn't take too kindly to your favor," Monty said. "I doubt it was the removal of the Golden Circle that spurred them into this reaction. More likely, it was the loss of face that you created. One mage usurping an entire sect from the Grand Council makes them look weak."

"They *are* weak, and the weak can never forgive, only the strong have that capacity," Dex said. "Understand, they will not let this perceived slight go unanswered. Remember that. You can't reason with them, or her. You can't appeal to their better nature or sense of justice, their moral compass is broken and corrupted by centuries of unchecked power. Their Emissary is an extension of this belief system. To face her is to face the Grand Council. In their minds, the Grand Council acts with impunity. They believe they are above all mages and answer only to themselves. Is this clear?"

I nodded.

"Thank you, Dex."

He clapped me on the shoulder and grinned again.

"Don't thank me yet," he said. "I am impressed with the both of you, though. You've made a better class of enemy. To think you've gotten the attention of the Grand Council; it makes an old mage proud."

I gave him a strange look, realizing that he and Kali were more alike than I imagined.

"You're actually proud the Grand Council wants to wipe us off the face of the earth?" I asked. It was slightly surprising, but not unexpected. He was the Harbinger of Death after all. "This is what makes you proud? We have a better caliber of enemy?"

"You can always judge a man by the quality of his enemies," Dex said. "Go find H. Get stronger. Give that Salya a lesson she won't forget. You can thank me by removing her as a threat. Get going."

He walked us to the entrance of the Main Building and then left.

We headed downstairs.

ELEVEN

We took the wide, marble staircase downstairs to the lowest level of the Main Building. We weren't actually on the lowest level but one level below the lowest level.

I'd say we were in the basement, but this level was closer to a sub-level with reinforced walls inscribed with runes of power. It felt more like entering a bunker than a basement.

"Who puts a library in a reinforced bunker?" I asked as we reached the lowest level. "This makes no sense. What kind of library requires this kind of security?"

That's when I looked around and noticed the circles.

"Those look like—"

"Obliteration circles?" Monty answered. "They just appear that way. I think it's my uncle's way of keeping the future students alert to their surroundings."

"If I was a student here, that would certainly do it," I said, eyeing the softly glowing circles. "Are you saying they aren't dangerous? These look almost exactly like the circles Julien has around his property."

"Almost exactly," Monty agreed. "My uncle made some subtle modifications that neutralize the lethality but enhance the teleportation aspect of these circles. Stepping in one would result in an instantaneous trip across the school grounds. Knowing my uncle, I'm sure it would be unpleasant —hold on."

He crouched down and examined one of the circles.

"This one"—he pointed to the circle in front of him— "will transport you directly to the Head Dean's office. I'm fairly certain that would end badly for the student."

"Head Dean?" I asked. "The Morrigan?"

He nodded.

"I would assume that to be the case."

"Dex is just evil," I said with a smile and shook my head. "I'm sure the other circles are just as bad."

Monty gave the other circles a quick scan and shook his head.

"I can confirm that all of these circles would lead to unpleasant adventures for the unfortunate student careless enough to activate them."

"I guess that's one way to teach situational awareness," I said, still eyeing the circles. "It is a school of battlemagic."

"Indeed," Monty said, leading us to the last the door on the right. "Care to read where we're going? This should answer your question."

He pointed to the symbols on the door.

I stood in front of the door and examined the symbols. At first, they were just a jumble of lines, until I used my innersight. Understanding flooded my brain. It wasn't as if I could read the symbols, it was closer to an instant comprehension of what the symbols meant.

When I looked at the symbols, it became clear.

We were headed to the Living Library.

"Ziller approved a doorway to the Living Library, here?" I asked, surprised. "This is a stolen sect and Dex is a magus non grata under an edict from the Grand Council. Isn't he going to catch some backlash by providing the school access to the library?"

"The Living Library falls under the jurisdiction of none of the governing bodies of the magical community," Monty said. "Besides, who is going to curtail what Professor Ziller does with the Library? I'd like to see the Grand Council try to enforce some rule on him. It would end badly for them."

"Ziller is stronger than the Grand Council?" I asked. "The *entire* Grand Council?"

"Ziller is not an average mage," Monty replied as he touched the symbols on the door in a specific sequence. That's when I noticed the door was Australian Buloke. When I looked at it carefully, I saw that it was a smaller version of the enormous door to the back room at the Randy Rump. "I don't know how old he is, but if the adage of knowledge being power is true, I'd have to say he is one of the most powerful mages alive."

The runes flared to life slowly with orange energy grew in intensity, one by one, in the order Monty had activated them. I could grasp the general idea behind the runes—they gave off a feeling of warning and access.

It was hard to understand.

Basically, I had the sense that even though Monty had used the right sequence, we needed to be careful going through this door. The access we had was reserved for a chosen few.

It felt like entering an area of classified materials. You knew the space was special, even if you had the clearance to be there. That's how this felt. We were entering a classified area off-limits to almost everyone.

I wondered if the Living Library was only for the instructors. The question must have shown itself on my face, because Monty answered me a second later.

"This is the faculty access to the Library," Monty said.

"The students will have another entrance on one of the upper levels. This entrance will be for the instructors."

"Instructor access only?" I asked. "Does that mean you're—?"

"We both have instructor access," he said. "You do recall what the Morrigan said?"

"I try not to dwell too much on what she says most of the time," I said, watching the symbols on the door rearrange themselves. "Her conversations hover between fearsome and terrorizing most of the time."

He nodded.

"She does have that effect," he said as the door slowly opened inward. "Let's go, Professor Ziller will be expecting us."

"How?" I asked. "We just got here."

"You tell me," he said. "How would he know to expect us?"

I looked at the door again and read one of the runes Monty had activated. It was clearly some kind of announcing rune.

"The runes," I said, pointing to the specific rune. "That one is like an early warning system. It lets anyone inside know who is accessing the Library."

"Not anyone, Professor Ziller," Monty said. "These runes will alert him which entrance is being activated and by whom."

"That's a lot of information," I said, examining the runes. "How do they do that?"

"You've just started really reading runes and now you would like me to explain their construction?" he said, glancing at me as he pushed the door further open. "I don't think I know enough of their construction to explain the concept in terms you would be able to understand. Ask

Professor Ziller, I'm sure he could explain it to you in simple terms."

I nodded.

"I will," I said "At some point I have to learn how to make them, right?"

"I don't know," Monty said as we stepped past the door into a long, white marble corridor. The door closed silently behind us. "You don't gesture or use runes when you execute your magic missile or darkflame. I see no reason you would need to use runes in the future for your abilities."

I gave it thought.

He was right.

I didn't need to do any finger-wiggles or actual runes when I unleashed my energy blasts or my dawnward. Probably because I wasn't a mage. I wondered if adding runes to the mix would make my dawnward stronger or my magic missile more powerful?

Was there a way to add more life-force to my dawnward or magic missile? My darkflame was strong. If I could add more of my life-force to it, could I make it stronger?

I'd have to ask Professor Ziller if runes could enhance my using my life-force, or if they would act as a barrier against my using the energy I could access. Surprisingly my brain wasn't hurting, even though I was positive I was having magey thoughts.

All around us off the actual corridor, I saw small alcoves with desks and comfortable chairs. I figured these alcoves were designed for study. In the center of the corridor we walked down, a deep golden runner of thick carpet covered the marble floor.

What I thought were Persian motifs were actually interlocking runes throughout the design. The runes served an interesting purpose. They helped create an aura of tranquility and peace. They weren't glowing or doing anything overt, but

I could sense a passive energy coming from the runner as we walked.

"The runes in the runner help this space feel peaceful," I said, looking down at the runner. "These alcoves—"

"Are for reading borrowed texts," Monty said. "Yes, the runes in the runners work passively to create a certain ambience in this space. I'm certain Ziller wove them into the runner himself. Well done on noticing the effects of the runes."

"Thanks," I said. "How powerful can they get?"

"You know the answer to that," Monty said, glancing back at me. "How overwhelming does Nemain feel when wielded?"

"Those are the runes?"

"Mostly, yes," he said with a nod. "Granted, those runes are difficult to inscribe and they also have a particularly detrimental side effect."

"They drive the user of the weapon insane," I said. "Are there such things as evil runes?"

Peaches bumped into my leg and I turned to glance down at him, wondering about the runes that occasionally appeared on his flanks.

"Evil runes?" Monty asked. "I don't think so. Words have power, but you know my position on the power we wield. I think runes fall into the same category. They have power, but that power is neutral. It depends on how it's wielded."

"The runes on Nemain do not feel neutral," I said, thinking about how that weapon made me feel. "They don't exactly feel evil, but they don't make me feel all warm and fuzzy either."

"Nemain is a weapon of death," Monty answered after a brief pause. "I would find it highly suspect for that weapon to make anyone feel warm and fuzzy. If you are truly curious about the runes on weapons, you should start with your own."

"My own?" I asked as we reached a junction and Monty took the left corridor. "What do you mean?"

"Doesn't Ebonsoul contain runes?"

"Well, yes," I said, taken off-guard. "I mean I never really read them. I couldn't decipher them."

"You should be able to now," he said. "It may be wise to know exactly what the weapon you're bonded to has inscribed on its blade. Don't you think?"

"You make a good point."

"I usually do," he said and stopped suddenly. "Our host is here."

"Ziller?" I asked, looking around. "Where?"

"Around the corner," Monty said. "That's odd, I thought he'd come out to greet us."

"Maybe he's busy?"

"Let's find out."

We walked to the end of the corridor and saw Ziller busy searching for something in a large bookcase filled with books. At a table nearby sat another person with his back to us, but I knew who it was almost immediately.

The white shirt and black vest were subtle clues, but it was the large egg cream and massive pastrami sandwich on the plate in front of him that really gave it away.

Ezra.

TWELVE

"Ezra?" I asked as he turned to face us. "You're here?"

"I am," Ezra said with a nod and a smile. "I'm never too far away from anywhere. The question is what are *you* doing here? Are you in search of a book?"

"Not really," I said as my hellhound padded over to Ezra and nuzzled his hand. "Peaches, behave."

"He is behaving exactly as a hellhound should," Ezra said, with a shooing motion before reaching down to rub my massive hellhound's head a few times. "I'm sure he must be hungry, hellhounds are always hungry."

Ezra reached under the table and produced an enormous titanium bowl with a large P inscribed on the side. The bowl was filled with some of the most appealing pastrami I had ever seen.

He placed the bowl on the floor next to the table and patted Peaches on the head.

Peaches sniffed the bowl a few times and it was as if a fountain of drool had been activated. He turned to face me and nearly drooled on me with a gob of saliva.

<*It's meat from the place! This is the best meat! The old man who*

smells like home is the best. I should eat it. He would feel bad if I didn't eat it. Can I eat it now? I'm starving.>

<You are not starving, but you should go ahead and eat it, boy. He brought it for you. Don't forget to thank him.>

Peaches approached the bowl and paused in front of Ezra. He lowered his head nearly to the floor and unleashed a low half-growl, semi-bark which shook the library.

"He's getting much stronger," Ziller said. "Are you sure he's still a pup?"

"He recently discovered his battleform," Ezra said, then glanced at me. "His bondmate is lagging somewhat it seems."

"Battleforms aren't easy, you know," I said, defending myself. "I didn't even know he had one until recently. Then I find out *his* battleform is really *our* battleform."

"Battleforms are always shared," Ezra explained. "You are bondmates, it's to be expected."

Ziller nodded.

"From my understanding, battleforms can be quite difficult to master," Ziller said, "if they don't kill you first. That does, however, explain the increase in his power."

"What was that about the battleform killing me?"

"Nothing you need to be concerned with," Ezra said. "Is your hound not hungry? He hasn't touched his meat."

"He wants to thank you first."

"Ah," Ezra said with a slight nod. "Of course, proper etiquette must be observed."

Peaches let out another low rumble and nuzzled Ezra's hand again.

"You are very welcome," Ezra said, patting my hellhound on the head again. "Make sure you eat it all. You're still a growing pup."

Peaches didn't need to be told twice. He proceeded to devour the pastrami in the bowl.

<Slow down, I don't think this meat will reappear like Kali's. Take it slow and enjoy the meat.>

<I'm still enjoying it, even if I eat it fast. Meat is joy, slow or fast.>

Another moment of profound wisdom from my enlightened ZenMaster hellhound. I shook my head and refocused on Ziller who was still searching in the bookcase.

"I'll be right with you," Ziller called out. "Give me a moment."

Ziller was dressed in his usual librarian casual look—jeans, a long sleeve white shirt, and construction boots. His sandy-brown hair was considerably longer this time and pulled back in a loose ponytail, probably so he could see the books in the bookcases, and what used to be a goatee was now a thick, full beard with more salt than pepper.

He still sported the rune-covered monocle over one eye. I noticed it had a soft violet glow around the lens as he searched the bookcase for what I guessed was a special book for Ezra.

"What is he searching for?" I asked, glancing at Ezra. "A book for you?"

Ezra nodded.

"Are you boys hungry?" Ezra asked. "I could whip up a little something if you're feeling peckish."

I raised a hand and politely shook my head, doing my best to decline the kind offer. Ezra's idea of a *little* something was a pastrami sandwich large enough to feed a hellhound. I don't think I could ever be that hungry at one time, not without fasting for a few weeks.

"No, thank you," Monty said. "We are a little pressed for time."

"Are you now?" Ezra asked, raising an eyebrow at Monty. "James, come attend to the boys. They seem to be in a bit of a rush. You've been looking for hours and you still haven't found it; it's not going to suddenly appear now."

"What exactly *are* you looking for, Professor Ziller?" Monty asked. "You've misplaced a book?"

Ziller glanced at Ezra with a small smile.

"Ezra would like to study the unique Lead Designer's Manual," Ziller answered. "*How to Design Yesterday, Tomorrow—Notes from a Lead Designer's Thoughts on Quantum Entanglement & Temporal Unraveling.* There's only one copy in existence on this plane."

"Written by the esteemed Professor himself," Ezra added. "James, I think the issue with the location of the book in question is that you didn't fix it in time—that temporal unraveling will make it impossible to locate when it is."

"I'm afraid you're correct," Ziller said with a nod, removing the monocle from his eye. "I'll have to ask Sid to step adjacent to our current timeline and see if he can locate it for me. If you're willing to wait."

"I have an abundance of time. That should be simple enough," Ezra said, waving him closer. "It would be good to see Sid again. I'd like to have some words with him. In the meantime, it seems there is a matter of some urgency here. Come see what's needed."

Ziller stepped closer to us.

By this point, we were all standing around Ezra. I think he had a natural gravitational pull. It seemed that wherever he was, he was the center of whatever was happening.

It didn't hurt that he was Death personified and likely the most powerful being wherever he was. Power like that defied any kind of explanation.

It just was.

"How can I help you?" Ziller asked. "I see you used the entrance at the School of Battlemagic. It's still under construction, but I think it's coming along nicely."

"It's looking good, but I have a question," I said. "Isn't providing access to the library and helping us going to catch you heat from the Grand Council? I'd hate for them to come after you. We have been designated outcasts, especially Dex."

"I heard," Ziller said. "To be designated outcasts, by the Grand Council no less; I must say I'm impressed."

"You're impressed?" I asked, incredulous. "You're not concerned they could act against you?"

"Against *me*?" He shook his head. "Unlikely. The Living Library predates the Grand Council by several millennia. It was old when the Grand Council was still a concept. Neither I, nor the Library have anything to fear from the Grand Council. Although, I have to say your concern is appreciated, but I'm not the one in danger here—you two are."

"True," Ezra said with a nod. "You have a formidable enemy hunting you now. You must be excited."

I stared at the both of them, the shock slowly running through my brain. They expected me to be excited and thrilled at the fact that the Grand Council was after us.

"Am I missing something here?" I said, confused. "I am not excited, or thrilled, or overjoyed that the Grand Council and this insane Emissary with her spear of death is after us. They want to erase and eliminate Monty, Peaches, and me."

"It's the Grand Council," Ziller said as if that was explanation enough. "Erase and eliminate is sort of their thing. Has been for centuries."

"What are you then?" Ezra asked calmly. "Surely you must be feeling something."

"I'm angry," I said after giving it a moment of thought. "I'm angry that the Grand Council thinks they can just act without there being any consequences to their actions. They think they can just erase and eliminate us and no one is going to call them on it."

"They have power," Ezra said as Ziller nodded. "People with power usually act without concern for consequences."

"Not this time," I said. "This time we're going to stop them."

"Why?"

"I don't understand, what do you mean—why?"

"Why are *you* going to stop them, aside from the obvious self-preservation," Ezra asked. "What is *your* motivation?"

"Keeping the people in my life alive is plenty of motivation," I said, not seeing where he was going with these questions. "I don't follow."

"That's plenty of motivation for you to save those in your life, true," Ezra answered, looking into my eyes. "You, however, are not in any *real* danger, are you, *Deathless*?"

Hearing him use that name threw me for a moment.

"I don't understand."

"You will," Ezra said with a nod. "Ziller, give them the assistance they need. Let's get them on their way."

Ziller produced a pen and paper.

"Book, message, or document?" Ziller asked. "Which were you given?"

"How did you know—?"

"It always comes down to one of those."

"Document," Monty said and looked at me. "Tell him."

I nodded and reached into my memory to retrieve the words from the document the Morrigan had given me. The words came to me instantly and I wondered if this was an effect of my unlocking my ability to read runes.

"This was what the Morrigan gave me:

Beneath the temple of Athena, when Selene's chariot is at its height, the doorway to the undying mage's domain will appear. To gain entrance, you must walk with Hades, but he must not have sway over you. With Charon's obol, all doors will open to you—choose wisely. Those who cling to life, die. Those who cling to death, live."

THIRTEEN

"It's so good to hear someone using the classics," Ezra said with a smile. "This one is quite clever. How far have you gotten, Tristan?"

"Not very," Monty said, shaking his head. "Some of it seems clear, but the passage is all broken apart like pieces of a puzzle I can't connect."

"Simon?" Ezra asked, glancing at me. "Were you able to decipher any of it?"

"I know who Athena, Hades, and Charon are. I'm guessing the undying mage is the Hidden Hand," I said. "The rest of it...I don't know. It doesn't make sense to me at all."

Ezra nodded.

"Some of it is obscure," Ezra said. "I'm sure Professor Ziller will be able to assist with this passage."

"Have you two compared notes?" Ziller asked. "Tristan, Simon, tell me, what you have uncovered from this passage?"

"Athena's temple, I'm assuming is the Parthenon," Monty said. "I was not aware of any portal access beneath it."

"There are several," Ziller said, pulling out a book from

one of the bookcases and placing it on a nearby table. "The passage informs you which portal to use."

"Selene's chariot," Monty said. "If it's at its height, it must mean a—"

"A full moon?" I volunteered. "Right?"

"Not bad," Monty said with a nod, even Ziller nodded approvingly. "You know your mythology."

"Not like I've had much of a choice, lately," I said. "I've been brushing up, but there are so many god groups."

"Pantheons," Monty corrected. "We don't call them god groups."

"Divine gangs?" I offered. "That's really what they act like."

"He's not exactly wrong," Ezra said. "Their behavior leaves much to be desired most of the time."

"Okay," I said. "We need to be at the Parthenon during the full moon to look for a door?"

"Not just *any* door," Ziller said with a hint of excitement in his voice. "You need to locate the Lunatic's Passage."

"The Door to Madness," Ezra added. "It's a difficult door to find."

"Aside from the fact that this door is not giving off 'come find me' vibes with that name, why is it difficult to locate?"

"It appears the doorway is only accessible for a short time," Ziller said, looking through the book he had pulled out. "But that's not the issue; it's the actual location of where it appears at the temple that makes it difficult."

"Where does it appear?" Monty asked. "How difficult is it to access?"

Ziller pointed to a map in the book.

Monty looked over and cursed under his breath.

"Are you certain?" Monty asked. "It's there, in that wall?"

Ziller nodded as I stepped over to take a look. He was pointing at a map of the Parthenon. The temple sat on a hilltop with smaller buildings surrounding it. The hilltop itself was flat and the dominating feature was the Parthenon.

Around the edge of the flattened hilltop, a wall had been built. I imagined this wall was ancient. In several locations around the top of the hill, this wall dropped down several hundred feet in some places into raw stone.

Ziller was pointing to a section of the wall to the south of the actual Parthenon. I leaned in and saw a runic symbol meaning the moon door.

"You're kidding," I said, examining the area. "This doorway appears in the wall?"

"For about ten minutes, every full moon," Ziller said. "That is not the Lunatic's Passage though. That's the beginning of the Passage."

"What?" I asked, looking at him. "It's not? That's not the door we need?"

"That's the door that leads to the corridor, that leads to the hall you need," he answered. "The Moon Hall will hold the entrance to the Lunatic's Passage."

"You're serious?"

"You didn't think it would be that easy, did you?" Ziller said. "Still, you need to be careful, that corridor is a force multiplier."

"Bloody hell," Monty said. "We can't let anything hit us."

Ziller nodded.

"You should be able to deal with any mages that manage to follow," Ziller said. "If Salya catches up to you in there... well. Close quarters with no place to go. It means you'll be meeting Ezra a lot sooner than you anticipated."

"No, thanks," I said, glancing at Ezra. "No offense."

"None taken," Ezra said. "Past the entrance corridor should be the first part of the Moon Hall. Once in there, the entrance will close behind you."

"That's when the Lunatic's Passage opens?"

"No, that would still be too simple," Ziller answered. "The Moon Hall holds the doors to the Lunatic's Passage. Try not to fight the Emissary here either."

"Is it another force multiplier?" I asked. "What is with this place?"

"Not a force multiplier, but a temporal trap," Ziller explained. "The solution is relatively simple; you need to leave before you arrive."

"The usual solution," Monty said with a nod. "This is a typical trap."

"Yes, but be mindful, she will know the way to escape it as well," Ziller said. "You must not waste time. After the Moon Hall you will find the entrances to the Lunatic's Passage. To gain access you must open the correct door."

"How do we do that?"

"You need the key."

"We need a key?"

"Correct," Ziller said. "You will have a small window. At most you will have two tries. Do not make a mistake."

"What happens if we make a mistake?" I asked because something told me we would be doing all of this under pressure. "Just in case."

"If you open the wrong door," Ziller said. "You will find yourself in Tartarus."

"Tartarsauce? The old god?" I asked. "He's down there?"

"The place, not the god," Monty said. "We do not want to go there...ever."

"The place," I said. "And the god?"

"As far as I know he is not down there," Ziller said. "That doesn't mean you want to visit the place. Open the correct door and you should be in Naxos, the Spartan's domain."

"There's another Naxos?" I asked.

"Yes, the one on your plane is a beautiful Greek Island," Ziller said. "The one inhabited by the Spartan is a separate plane under his control. As I understand it, it is also quite beautiful and resembles the island near Greece."

"But *that* Naxos belongs to the Spartan, right?"

"Yes," Ziller said. "See? Not that complicated."

I stared at him.

"Not that simple, but it could have been worse."

"Right," I said, glancing down at the map again. "Why would the initial entrance be a corridor that appears in the middle of a sheer wall hundreds of feet above the ground? With no obvious method of access, *that* would be too easy."

"Exactly," Ziller said with a nod. "According to the written passage, I believe you have everything else you need, except the obol."

"We need a ball?" I asked, trying to understand what he was suggesting. "Why do we need a ball? What kind of ball?"

"Obol," Ziller said, heading back to the bookcase. "Not a ball, an obol, specifically, Charon's obol."

I glanced at Monty.

"If he starts with Who's on first, I'm leaving."

"An obol," Ziller started, putting on his monocle, while looking through the shelves, "is a specific coin, placed in the mouth of the recently deceased. It's an ancient tradition dating back at least to the 5th century BC."

"Charon's obol?" I said, thinking about the term. "You mean according to this custom the dead had to *pay* to get into the Underworld? Dying itself wasn't enough? There was a cover charge?"

"When you put it in those terms, well, yes," Ziller admitted. "It was the custom of the time."

"How did they know what coin to use?" I asked, shaking my head. "What if it was too much? Did Charon have to carry change?"

"It needs to be a low denomination coin," Ziller answered,

taking me seriously—academics had a strange sense of humor. "I think I have one here. One moment."

"He's serious?" I asked, glancing at Monty again. "We really need this obol? Can't I just use a quarter or a dime?"

"I think it's best we stick with tradition for this," Monty said. "If he has an obol, we'll use it."

"What happened if the recently deceased didn't have an obol?" I asked. "Sometimes you leave home without change, and meet Ezra on the way to the market. Oops, now you're dead with no obols. Would Charon send them back with a stamp of some kind: something like 'insufficient funds'? Did they then get to be alive again?"

"I think you're reading too much into this, Simon," Monty said, slightly irritated. "The obol is part of a tradition, and may be instrumental in opening the door we need. If you want to pursue the deeper significance of this tradition, I'm sure Hades could arrange a meeting with Charon, and you could ask him all the questions you'd like."

"I'm good," I said, raising a hand in surrender. "No need to get snippy. I was just curious about the whole obol thing. It seems unnecessary."

"Actually, we still practice many customs that may seem unnecessary, but are rooted in ancient beliefs. Especially, when it comes to the burial rites of the dead."

I gave him a look, because I knew what was coming next. We were standing in the Living Library and Ziller was a few feet away. There was no way Monty was going to be able to resist entering professor mode.

It was impossible.

"I wasn't aware," I said, surrendering to the inevitable. "But I am positive you're going to share some of these rituals with me, aren't you?"

"There's the *prothesis*, which was the laying out of the body, or what we call the wake, then there's the funeral procession, known as the *ekphora*, and finally, the interment or cremation of the body, all of which are practices that originated in ancient Greece, that are still being practiced today."

"Imagine that," I said, shaking my head. "The tradition is still going after hundreds, no, thousands of years. That is incredible."

"Stop being facetious," Monty said, chastising me. "You need to know about these traditions. We don't know if it will figure in locating H."

He was right, of course.

"Okay as far as we know, according to the passage, all doors will open to whoever has Charon's obol. Does that mean some kind of payment needs to be made?"

"I don't know," Monty said. "I figure we will find out once we get there."

"Do you know?" I asked, turning to Ezra. "More importantly, would you tell us if you did know?"

Ezra smiled.

"I always knew you were clever," Ezra said, tapping the side of his nose. "The answer to your questions are no, and no, but one of those is a lie. You get to figure out which is which."

I just stared at him.

It didn't matter. He wasn't going to give us the right answer either way. We were going to have to figure it out, once we were on site.

"Here we go," Ziller said, holding up a small coin he must have dug up from the pile of books he had been looking through. "This is an obol. I don't know if it's the one you need, but it's an obol from the right time period."

"You said we had everything we needed, except the obol," I said. "What about that whole part about walking with Hades?"

"You have that answer," Ziller said, pointing at me and handing the obol to Monty. "Actually *you* are that answer."

"Excuse me?"

"You walk with Hades in more ways than one," Ezra said. "Pointing at Peaches."

"My hellhound?" I asked in disbelief. "That means I walk with Hades?"

"You must walk with Hades, but he must not have sway over you," Monty said, completing that part of the passage. "You're bonded to a hellhound, but you will never enter the Underworld, at least not the conventional way. Hades has no sway over you."

"In a very twisted way, that makes sense. What about that last part about clinging to life and death?" I asked, looking from Monty to Ezra and ending on Ziller. "Anyone have an answer for that?"

"*That* is an actual puzzle," Ezra said with a nod. "The only point of reference for using that passage would be Matthew 10:39."

"The biblical verse?"

"Don't be a *schlemiel*." Ezra tapped me not so lightly on the forehead with a finger. "How many references to *Matthew* do you know outside of biblical verse?" he asked. "Is there another Matthew out there that gets referred to this way? Of course, the biblical verse."

I refrained from making a comment because, well, it wasn't exactly a smart idea giving Death attitude. I had a feeling that despite Kali's curse, he could probably make my death stick.

Not that I actually wanted to find out.

"Then we *do* have everything we need," I said, rubbing my forehead. Even though he appeared to be an old Jewish scholar, he had phenomenally strong fingers. "We should get going, then."

"Yes, you should," Ezra said with a nod. "Ziller, can you provide them with a door?"

Ziller nodded.

"Right this way," Ziller said, pointing to a corridor. "You can leave immediately."

"Before we go, I do have one question," I said, undeterred as I turned back to look at Ezra. "The Archangel Metatron, do you know him?"

Ezra narrowed his eyes, smiled, and tapped the side of his nose before pointing at me.

"There's still hope for you yet," he said. "To answer your question, yes."

"You do?" I asked surprised. "Really?"

"Now, no more questions," he said waving me on. "You two need to be a pair of menschen. You have an Emissary to face, and a Grand Council to thwart."

Monty gave me a look and shook his head.

"Thank you, Ezra," Monty said. "Your assistance has been invaluable."

"Think nothing of it," Ezra said. "Remember not to take everything so literally."

Monty nodded as Ziller gently ushered us into a corridor. I looked back and saw my hellhound give Ezra another nuzzle, before bounding after me.

"That was risky," Monty said as Ziller led us down the corridor. "What possessed you to ask him that?"

"I'd like to meet him one day," I said. "Know what I mean?"

"Meet who?"

"Metatron. I figured Ezra was the safest way to do that," I said. "I mean, maybe Ezra can make the call, and I can meet one of the most powerful archangels in existence."

"Or get yourself blasted to particles," Monty added, shaking his head. "I'd consider waiting a few centuries before you meet him. Hopefully, by then you would have learned to temper your comments with some wisdom."

"We'll see," I said with a smile. "Wisdom can be overrated."

"Here we are," Ziller said, pointing to what appeared to be an ordinary wooden door. "This doorway will lead you to a restaurant near the Parthenon."

"Do we know what phase the moon is in over Greece?" I asked as Ziller touched parts of the door. "Are we going to have to sit there for days, waiting for a full moon?"

"Simon..."

"What, I think that's a valid question."

"The moon will be full at nightfall," Ziller said, pulling out a timepiece from his pocket. "Greece is seven hours ahead of us, presently. Seeing as how it's only four p.m. there at this moment, you have until six p.m. or sunset before the moon rises. Do you recall the location of the portal that leads to the Lunatic's Passage?"

Monty and I both nodded.

"I'm still not a fan of this passage," I said. "Couldn't they have named it something less threatening?"

"If you choose the wrong passage, you will understand why it was given that name," he said. "Make sure you choose the correct door."

"I have a fairly accurate idea of what will indicate the correct passage," Monty said. "Especially if it's rooted in Matthew 10:39."

"Good," Ziller said. "Remember the historical iconography of the time."

Monty nodded.

"I'm glad *you* have some idea," I said, before looking at Ziller. "Should we expect much resistance?"

"The Emissary will try to intercept you after you access the entrance," Ziller answered. "She will not be alone."

"I thought she only worked alone because she was so deadly?"

"She does, but she won't *be* alone," he said. "She *will* engage you alone, rather than risk the cadre of mages that will be with her."

"That's comforting," I said. "How large will this cadre be?"

"I would expect a considerable number of Sanitizers and Verity agents, in and around the temple," he said. "Enough to present a sizable threat. They will be waiting."

"Where exactly does this door lead?" Monty asked. "How close to the temple?"

"This door will lead you to a nearby restaurant in the vicinity of the Parthenon, named Xenious Zeus. Once there, look for Mage Nicholas, or Nico. He's a member of the Living Library and will be able to assist you in approaching the Parthenon without being discovered."

"Are we placing him in danger?" Monty asked. "We don't want to risk his safety."

"Nico possesses a very unique skill—he is a chameleon," Ziller said. "Nico's purpose will be to conceal your energy signatures as best as possible. I'm afraid he won't be able to completely mask your signatures, but he should be able to buy you some time and access to the portal."

"A chameleon?" Monty asked. "I haven't encountered a chameleon in years."

"He is the assistant chef," Ziller said. "It shouldn't be too difficult to locate the restaurant. You won't notice him, but he will certainly notice you."

"How far away is this restaurant?"

"The restaurant is far enough away to be somewhat safe, but close enough to be walking distance from the temple," Ziller said. "Nico will be expecting you. Even so, be on your guard. The Grand Council will attempt to be preemptive."

"We shall be," Monty said. "Thank you again for your assistance."

Ziller nodded and pressed several sections of the door.

Orange and red runes came to life, glowing brightly with energy. As he opened the door, I felt a strong breeze across my face. In the distance, I could see the Parthenon lit by the setting sun.

"Remember the passage," Ziller said. "You have all the clues you need."

We walked through the door. A moment later, we were standing some distance from the columns of the Parthenon as the sun was beginning to set. Amazingly, my stomach didn't want to leap from my body. In fact, it was one of the smoothest teleports I had ever experienced.

"Let's move," Monty said. "We don't have much time."

"I'll take that teleport over one your teleportation circles any day," I said under my breath. "How did he do that?"

"Not even my uncle could match Ziller's power and teleportation ability," Monty said, looking around. "It would take me ages to create a temporal bridge that smooth."

The first thing I noticed was the security around the temple. In the distance I noticed the restaurant.

"It seems like the dinner crowd is just starting to gather," I said, looking at the interior of the restaurant. "Maybe we should head to the kitchen?"

"That would be prudent," Monty said, scanning the area. "Even here, there is an abundance of Grand Council mages in the area."

We made our way into the restaurant, and I saw a young man approach us with a nod. He was dressed in a white shirt and black pants.

There was nothing extraordinary about him, but I figured that was the point—he was supposed to blend in. He nodded in our direction before quickly gesturing and disappearing my hellhound.

I could still sense Peaches, but he was invisible to my sight. The young man led us to the back of the restaurant, while avoiding any of the patrons that were coming in.

"Nico?" Monty asked. "It's a pleasure to meet you."

"The pleasure is mine," Nico said. "Please come with me."

He motioned for us to follow him. Once we were away from the other customers, he gestured again, hiding Monty and me.

"Your skill is impressive," Monty said, keeping his voice low.

"Thank you," Nico said in a hushed tone. "We must move quickly."

"I'm afraid our hellhound will stand out, even with your camouflage. Can you lead us to the temple while keeping us hidden?"

Nico nodded.

"Sanitizers have flooded the area," he said. "So far the Emissary hasn't arrived. We need to leave before she does."

"Can you keep us hidden until then?" I asked, looking around the restaurant. "This place is getting crowded with mages."

"They started arriving a few hours ago," he said, "Fortunately, there is no Emissary."

"Agreed," Monty said. "We don't want to run into her. At least, not yet."

Nico nodded, but kept his face impassive as we moved through the restaurant to the rear entrance.

"I will do my best," Nico said, keeping his voice low and looking around. "All three of you will be nearly impossible to hide for longer than ten minutes or so—your energy signatures are too strong. I need to get you to the Parthenon as quickly as possible. Come with me."

I scanned the area as we moved quickly down the streets.

We stayed close to Nico as he guided us out of the restaurant and onto the side streets, away from the evening dinner crowd filled with tourists.

Even though I couldn't see him, I could sense Monty close by. I knew that if I could sense him, Salya would be able to sense us too.

"We really need to get out of here," I said. "This is a massacre waiting to happen."

"The Parthenon is a short distance way," Nico said. "I will create simulacra to buy you some time. I must leave you now."

Nico headed off in the opposite direction. I sensed the simulacra he created and was nearly fooled. It felt exactly like Monty and Peaches were down the street. I couldn't sense myself, however.

"He has exceptional skill," Monty said as we approached the hilltop where the Parthenon sat. "Even I would assume we were heading away from the temple."

I scanned the area again. From the way they were dressed, I noticed there were fewer tourists and more Sanitizers in the area around the Parthenon.

"They don't know what to look for," I said, keeping my voice low. "How close are we to sunset?"

"The Sanitizers may not know what to look for, but I can assure you, the Emissary will be searching for us," he said. "We need to move before Nico's signature mask wears off."

"Monty, I'm aware there's an actual security detail," I said. "Considering that the Parthenon is on the UNESCO World Heritage List, it makes sense that they would have a large security detail. What doesn't make sense is the—"

"Large amount of mages that have filled the ranks of the normal security detail?" Monty finished. "It would seem the

Grand Council has added a substantial number of mages, specifically Sanitizers."

"We need to be careful," I said. "The last thing we want to do is to destroy parts of the Parthenon. I have a feeling the mage authorities of Greece would be beyond upset if we blew up parts of this place."

"Agreed," Monty said. "Currently, I'm not sensing Emissary Salya, which means they won't act until sunset. In the meantime, we need to get off this hilltop and position ourselves in proximity to the anticipated location of the portal. Any destruction that occurs will be placed squarely on our shoulders."

"Wonderful," I said. "I doubt the Emissary will be concerned about damage to the Parthenon."

It was in that moment, that Nico's mask dropped.

FOURTEEN

There were still some tourists milling around the temple itself.

Monty and I moved to join the crowd that was standing around the temple grounds. We mingled with one large group and then shifted to another. Most of the people were okay with my hellhound, as long as we didn't get too close.

There was only one small problem.

The crowds were thinning out.

From what I could see, the temple closed in about thirty minutes. I noticed the tourists were filing out of the temple grounds; the Sanitizers, not so much.

"They're not leaving the temple grounds," I said, admiring the temple as some of the far spotlights came on. "If we stay here much longer, it's just going to be us, the Grand Council, and Verity Agents. Not exactly my idea of a fun evening."

"According to the posted signs, we have about thirty minutes," Monty said, looking up at the evening moon. "From the looks of that moon, the portal should be appearing any moment."

Monty scanned the south wall and started heading to where we needed to go. I took a step back to admire the Parthenon in all its majesty. I could only imagine what it had looked like when it was originally constructed.

The view was spectacular as the lights came on and illuminated the temple. It was truly a staggering sight of majesty and incredible architecture.

"Okay," I said, following him. "I'm officially impressed. If we ever manage to go back in time, we're coming here. We can't blow this place up. When I say we, I mean you."

"Nor can we stay to admire the temple," Monty said, nudging me and pointing off to the side of the temple. "We need to get down there."

I looked down and saw the sheer drop as the moon began to rise.

"If you cast anything, these Sanitizers will be all over us," I said, glancing at the mages around us. "Actually, how are they not all over us right now?"

"I've managed to enhance Nico's mask to the extent that it still hides our signatures," he said as we walked over to the wall. "If I attempted to replicate the visible cloaking aspect, it would attract too much attention. That being said, I'm not as talented as a chameleon; this mask won't last much longer."

We headed over to the edge of the wall and looked down.

The portal hadn't appeared yet, but I sensed the energy building up beneath us. As the energy increased in power, I could tell it would only be a matter of minutes before the portal did appear.

"What happens if we miss the portal?"

"We get to have a prolonged and I'm fairly certain, violent, conversation with the Emissary about our presence here."

"Can't we be tourists enjoying the Parthenon?" I asked. "I've always wanted to visit."

"Considering your track record with demolitions, I highly doubt any of the mage groups in all of Greece want you near this building," Monty said under his voice. "Your reputation precedes you."

"*My* reputation?" I asked, incredulous. "You must be joking."

"I don't joke," he said, scanning the Sanitizers around us. "Did I tell you about the letter we received from the city?"

"Letter, what letter?"

"Sounded very official," he said. "From the Office of Engineering and Buildings as well as the Department of Parks."

"Department of Parks?" I asked. "Why would they be sending us letters?"

"It seems Ramirez is also involved with those agencies," Monty said. "It appears he would like to have some words about Little Island, specifically why it sank."

"I had nothing to do with that," I hissed. "That was all you magical people."

"Don't sell yourself short," Monty said with a small smile. "I seem to recall you being in the midst of the fray, along with the Echelon and all those other magical people."

"Only because I didn't have a choice."

"Simon, there is always a choice," he said, keeping his focus on the area below us on the wall. "I'm sure you've realized this by now."

"I have," I said, doing a little scanning of my own. "Do you have a plan on how to get down there? Because I'm not seeing stairs, a ramp, or an elevator."

"What we need is a distraction," Monty said. "Something that will call the Sanitizers away from this area and focus their attention on the other side of the hill."

"Something non-destructive, right?"

He remained silent for a few seconds as he looked off into the distance.

"Monty?" I pressed. "A non destructive distraction?"

"Hmm? Yes?" he said, glancing at me. "You were saying?"

"You're thinking of something non-destructive to get their attention, right?" I asked. "This is the Parthenon; it's not like we can slap on a new coat of paint or replace these columns. You understand the world of grief we will call down on ourselves if *you* obliterate any part of this temple, right? This place is beyond a landmark, this is a historical location."

"I'm aware," he said, eyeballing the columns. "We could have one column fall in a controlled implosion and—"

"Turn the place to rubble," I finished. "Are you insane? No column implosions, none."

Monty scanned the temple again.

"You do have a point," he said after a few seconds. "We're not here to destroy the temple and it may be structurally compromised."

"Oh really, a twenty-five hundred year old temple may be structurally compromised," I said. "Who would've imagined?"

"This is not the time for humor," he said, still focused on subtly examining the area over the edge. "I need you to get serious."

I glared at him.

For the briefest of seconds, I wondered what would happen if I helped him over the edge. Knowing him, he'd have some air cast that would stop him halfway down the wall. Handy in a pinch, when falling off a building, not so handy when surrounded by psychotic mages.

The urge to launch him into the stratosphere passed and I let out a deep breath.

"I'm so glad you got the memo," I said, pretending to point to something in the distance. "We do this without destroying the temple."

"In any case, there's plenty of rubble in the area," he said, turning and looking at the ground around the temple. "I'm not planning on adding any more. Besides, the temple structure is currently being restored. I would hate to undo all of that work."

I breathed out a sigh of relief.

"Still, I have to facilitate a method for us to access the portal when it appears," he added. "Can you convince your creature to be menacing in the far corner of the temple for exactly ten seconds, ten seconds from signal?"

"That's pretty precise," I said, glancing at Peaches. "I'm sure he can do it. How menacing?"

"Nothing dangerous," he said. "Perhaps he can make his eyes glow for a few seconds, maybe growl long enough to get their attention."

"A baleful glare?"

"Yes, exactly, something that looks menacing and dangerous," he said. "While he gets their attention, I'll create a teleportation circle to get us down there, I hope."

"A baleful glare looks dangerous because it is dangerous," I warned. "He can punch a hole through the stone with his omega beams. That would be bad."

"Depends on the stone. Can he do it?"

"This is risky," I said, crouching down next to my hellhound. "Won't they sense if you cast?"

"Yes," he said. "Especially the Verity Agents—these seem to be trackers. The distraction your creature creates, coupled with my speed should negate any attention I create."

"You didn't exactly sound certain you could pull off this teleportation circle to shift us to the portal mid-air," I said. "Can you?"

"Of course," he said. "We need to move now; it would appear the Grand Council is taking every precaution. More Verity Agents are on their way."

I nodded.

"Every precaution except sending the Emissary," I said, looking around. "Isn't that weird?"

"Weird, no. Troubling, yes," Monty said. "For now, I will take it as a stroke of good luck."

"Our luck has never been *that* good," I said, still scanning the area. We had moved away from the bulk of the Sanitizers, but the Verity agents were still near the area we needed cleared. "How are we going to move them?"

"Once you and your hound create the distraction, you leap over the edge," Monty said. "Are you ready?"

"You want me to what?"

"Was I unclear?" he asked. "You said it yourself, there are no stairs, ramps, or elevators. You wish to keep the temple intact—"

"Because it's the right thing to do?"

"That means a non-invasive method of entry," he said. "A distraction, followed by a quick exit over the edge. Actually, it's not that complicated."

"Your definition of complicated isn't matching mine, just so you know," I said. "This is getting more complicated by the second."

"If you and your hound would position yourselves over there, I will give you two signals—one to start the distraction and one to join me over the edge."

"You literally want me to just jump over the edge? Just like that?"

"Of course not," he said. "I expect the both of you to jump over the edge."

"Because that's so much better."

He pointed to the far corner of the hilltop, near a small temple.

"Over there. That should be perfect," he continued, pointing to a small structure on the far side. "You're in full view of the Sanitizers and Verity—perfect. You should go there, now."

I shook my head and walked over to the far corner of the hilltop. The Parthenon was to the side of me as I stood in front of a smaller temple dedicated to Athena Nike.

I guessed we were just going to do this.

I really hoped she lived up to her name, because we needed this operation to go off successfully. Monty remained where he was, with the Parthenon to his back as he looked down and over the edge of the southern wall.

I stood in front of Nike's temple and rubbed my hellhound's massive skull. I took a few breaths and calmed myself, making sure I had access to Grim Whisper. There was no way I was going to start flinging darkflame around any of these temples.

<Hey, boy. You see where Monty is standing?>

<Yes, why is he over there? He should come over here.>

<He needs to stay over there for now. Any second a door is going to appear in the wall underneath us.>

He looked down.

<Not here, over there, near Monty.>

<Why are we here? We should be over there.>

<We will be, but first, you see all these people?>

By now, all of the tourists had left, leaving only Sanitizers and Verity Agents. They had started giving Monty and me longer and longer looks.

We were running out of time.

Once that portal formed, we would be completely out of time.

<I see them. They smell different. Not good.>

<In a few seconds, they're going to want to attack us. We aren't going to let that happen. I need you to scare them before they attack.>

<Scare them? You want me to speak? That will scare them.>

<No! I mean, no, no speaking. We can't knock down any of these buildings. Can you use your omega beams?>

<You want me to hit them with my beams? That will hurt them.>

<No, don't hit them, at least not yet. Can you hit the ground next to that big group over there?>

<I can, for more meat from the place. Do you have more meat with you?>

I stared at my hellhound.

<You pick the worst times to negotiate. Can't you just hit the ground with your omega beams and scare them shitless?>

<You don't want me to just look in their direction and send my beams everywhere?>

<No! I mean, no, that would be bad. I need you to be precise with your beams. On the ground, in a precise controlled burst without hitting anyone. Can you do that?>

<I can, but that requires a precise controlled burst, that means I have to concentrate.>

<I hope you would concentrate, yes.>

<That means I'm going to need meat. You're asking for a cervical strike of my very specific and mighty eye beams. If you don't want me to miss, that requires some of the best meat. The meat from the place. Frank told me to always ask for things when I have to execute cervical strikes. He said that's when you need my beams the most. He said that's the best time to negotiate.>

I counted to ten, cursed the lizard a few times, keeping my breath and expression under control. Once I was done counting to ten, I did it again just to make sure.

<Surgical, not cervical, and I will take you to Ezra's and get you all the meat you can eat, if you could hit that big boulder next to the group without hitting any of those men. Think you can do it?>

He chuffed in response and entered 'beam and melt' mode, focusing on the boulder next to a group made up of Sanitizers and Verity Agents.

<I can. When?>

I glanced over at Monty who shook his head slightly.

<Not yet. Almost.>

I felt the surge of power form on the wall below Monty. I wasn't the only one who detected the spike of power, because most of the mages around us turned to look in Monty's direction.

He looked up and stared at me as he started gesturing.

"Now! Simon!"

<Do it, boy!>

The area around the Parthenon exploded with beams and debris as my hellhound unleashed his baleful glare at the ground in every direction.

The screams started almost immediately. I guessed Sanitizers and Verity Agents weren't used to facing off against hellhounds with omega beams.

They began running around, taking cover behind the temples and drawing their weapons. I noticed a lack of orbs flying around the temple grounds. It was a smart play. It seemed no one wanted to be responsible for causing damage to any of the structures on the hilltop.

I made sure Peaches and I took cover. There was no need to give the mages easy targets. I kept my eyes on Monty. That first signal was the distraction. He still had one more signal to send.

That would be the signal that let me know it was time exit the hilltop. I really hoped he had a plan to get us, not only to the portal but past the portal and into the Lunatic's Passage.

I was beginning to understand why it was named that way.

To his credit, Peaches didn't blast any of the mages.

That didn't mean he didn't look convincing. He moved methodically from group to group and blasted the ground, avoiding the Parthenon and anything that may have looked important.

I was really going to have to get him an enormous amount of meat for his precision. I felt another spike in energy. This one was stronger than the last one. I ran over to where Peaches stood.

I saw Monty leap over the edge.

<Follow Monty! Now!>

I felt Peaches latch onto my leg with his massive jaws and we blinked out from where we stood.

FIFTEEN

We blinked back in.

We were falling.

I looked down and saw the rocks below racing up to greet me. My hellhound whipped his head around and locked his gaze onto Monty. If Peaches was concerned about us falling, he gave no indication.

I felt him clamp down a bit harder on my leg.

We blinked out again.

A few seconds later, we blinked back in and fell right into a large green circle which yanked us sideways into another green circle which deposited us unceremoniously onto a smooth stone floor.

We were inside a cylindrical tunnel made of stone, the same stone that formed the Parthenon. The tunnel itself was glowing a soft gold and I could just make out the runes etched into the walls all around us.

Peaches landed gracefully while I sprawled onto the floor and slid for several feet, before coming to a stop. Ahead of us, I saw Monty moving fast.

"No time for a break!" he yelled. "This portal will close soon, let's go!"

I scrambled to my feet and began running.

Behind us, I sensed a group of energy signatures. Sanitizers and Verity Agents had dropped into the entrance after us. They were waiting and ready to give pursuit.

"We have company!" I yelled, drawing Grim Whisper. "You want me to convince them that following us is a bad idea? I have Persuaders loaded."

I aimed the gun behind me and let off one shot.

"No!" Monty yelled and came towards me. "Get down!"

I slid forward as Monty raced back and passed me, throwing up a golden lattice to block the passage. The Persuader round I had fired hit the lattice with force. More force than Grim Whisper usually packed.

"What was that?" I asked, looking at the lattice, then at Grim Whisper. "What happened?"

"This part of the Lunatic's Passage is the force multiplier," Monty said, moving forward again. "Anything fired down this passage is multiplied by several orders of magnitude."

"A heads-up would've been nice," I said, holstering Grim Whisper and picking up the pace. "Does that mean if they unleash orbs—?"

As if in on cue, several black energy orbs sailed past my head.

I heard them sizzle the air next to my head as they raced by.

I picked up the pace.

"They're flinging orbs, Monty!"

"We need to get to the next area before Salya arrives," he said. "Hurry, the passage will start closing soon."

"What are you talking about?" I asked. "Salya isn't down here."

"She will be," he said and headed onward. I raced to catch up. "Hurry."

"What do you mean?" I asked as I caught up to Monty. A low rumble traveled through the corridor, forcing me to look behind us. "What was that?"

"That was my lattice being ripped apart," Monty said. "Quickly, into the Moon Hall. Follow my every step and do as I do. Your creature will have to wait here."

"I don't understand—"

"We don't have time for you to understand, Simon," Monty said, his voice urgent. "Do as I do, now. Your hellhound stays here or we all die!"

<Wait here, boy. I'll be right back.>

<I go where you go.>

<Wait for me here. We'll be right back.>

Peaches chuffed and sat, staring at me.

<Come right back, bondmate.>

<I will, promise.>

Monty turned around and stepped backwards into the Moon Hall. He walked backwards to one of the nearby doors, opened the door and stepped through it backwards. I followed him exactly as he gestured and sealed the door in front of us.

Behind us was another door identical to the one we had just used. He gestured again and took us through that door the same way. Behind that door was one more door. Monty repeated the gesture and opened the door.

On the other side of this door I saw my hellhound, but we were approaching him from the back, which made no sense, since I had backed up from him to enter the first door.

Monty closed the door and gestured one more time, creating symbols which floated over to the door and remained hovering there.

Something looked odd about his gesture, then I realized what it was—he was doing his finger-wiggle in reverse order. The group of symbols that formed on the door looked familiar and strange at the same time. I tried to read them and discovered they were indecipherable.

"I can't read them," I said, looking at the symbols. "What happened? I was able to read them before."

"That's because you're trying to read them normally," he said, pointing at the symbols. "They're inverted, a mirror image, try again."

I looked at the symbols and saw that Monty was right, they were inverted. Once I realized what it was, I could make them out with some practice.

"It's a lock?" I asked. "You locked the door?"

"Yes," he said as we exited the door backwards. I nearly stepped on Peaches as we appeared behind him. "It's three locks—two I locked and one I left unlocked. That will buy us some time...I hope."

"Why would you leave one unlocked?"

"You tell me," he said as we moved into the Moon Hall. "Imagine a door with three locks. What would happen if I only locked two?"

I thought about the problem and it dawned on me.

"You are a devious mage," I said after a while. "She will be consistently locking one of the locks in an effort to open them all."

"That won't last long," Monty said, heading down another narrow corridor. "She's an Emissary. She will figure it out soon enough. We need to be gone by the time she gets through the entrance to the Moon Hall."

"She can follow us?" I asked looking at the door. "Even through this?"

"Especially through this," he said leading us to a narrow

corridor. "We're at the actual entrance to the Lunatic's Passage."

The narrow corridor led us down into an empty semicircular room. Along the wall on the far side of the room I saw five doors covered in cryptic runes. All of the doors were large slabs of wood. I figured they opened inward, since I didn't see any form of handle on the side I could see.

"No handles?" I asked. "Were they saving on materials?"

"They must push inward," Monty answered, looking around. "One of these doors leads to the Passage. It's the only thing that makes sense."

"Things stopped making sense a long time ago," I said, examining the surface of the doors. "I'm not expecting them to start making sense now."

"We must find the right door," he said, looking at several of the doors. "They look identical but there must be some difference. Check each one carefully."

The wood of the doors gave off an oppressive energy signature, as the runes themselves glowed a deep violet.

"Those are not normal runes," I said with a gasp as the pressure from the doors pressed on my chest. "What is this energy?"

"These...these are protorunes," Monty said with difficulty as he handed me the obol. He must have been feeling the pressure too. "Let's find the right door."

"How much time do we have before Salya finds us?"

"Not nearly long enough," he said. "Let's focus our energies on the door, not the Emissary. Examine the doors. See if there is anything out of the ordinary."

He moved off to examine the door on the far left, I moved to the door on the far right. It was difficult to stand too close to the doors because of their energy signatures, but I managed to get fairly close, close enough to make out the images on the doors.

"You're kidding," I said, pointing to my far right door. "Everything about this door is out of the ordinary; there's a skull in the middle of it, runic protoscript I can't read is covering every square inch, and this field with three crosses—"

"*Three* crosses?" Monty asked, turning to me. "Did you say three crosses?"

"Yes, look, all the doors have the same image, big cross in the middle two small crosses, one on each side, there"—I pointed to the corner—"right there, see it?"

"This door only has *two* crosses," Monty said, sliding over to the next door. "Same here. Check the rest of your doors."

"Check them for what?" I asked. "What does that even mean?"

"It means there's an anomaly," Monty said, coming over to my door. "This may be the difference we need."

"An extra cross?" I asked incredulous. "That's the difference we need?"

"That extra cross has a deeper meaning," he said. "The extra cross holds a profound significance."

"Profound significance?" I scoffed. "That's beyond reaching. I'll tell you what it means."

He glanced at me, raising an eyebrow at my response.

"Oh, you're going to put your years of study into ancient Greek carvings to good use?" Monty asked. "Would you, while you're at it, kindly decipher these protorunes, which are probably older than most of known civilization? I'd really appreciate it."

I glared at him.

"Mock all you want. I'll tell you what the extra cross means," I snapped. "It means that whoever was working on these doors probably discovered how hard this wood was after the first door."

"Without doubt," Monty said, tapping the door. "This

wood would probably give Australian Buloke a run for its money. It's as strong, if not stronger, than Buloke."

"See?" I said with a nod and a minor headache as the energy around me began to increase. "He probably said to himself: 'I'm not carving three crosses again, this wood feels like steel. Every door gets two crosses from now on, makes my life easier.'"

"A sound explanation," Monty said with a nod. "If the door with three crosses was the first door, why carve crosses into the following doors at all? Why not avoid them altogether?"

"Too noticeable. It was probably part of the contract," I said. "The doors had to have crosses. Two or three, he could get away with, not that big a deal. None? That would stand out."

"Most definitely."

I nodded.

"It was probably a non-union job, and he wasn't getting paid enough for three crosses per door." I continued. "Can't say I blame the guy. It's not easy standing here next to these doors. My head is beginning to pound."

Monty nodded and stepped close to my door, examining the corner with the crosses.

"As entertaining as your explanation was, I'm afraid it's incorrect," Monty said. "The door with the three crosses is the correct door."

"How exactly do you know that?" I asked, rubbing one of my temples. "Seriously, Monty, these doors are beginning to feel like a sledgehammer to my head."

"It's the runes," he said. "The sooner you deposit the obol, the sooner we can get past these doors, and put some distance between us and the Emissary."

"What if you're wrong?" I asked as I pinched the obol between my thumb and index finger. "What's behind door number one? An all-expenses paid, one-way trip to the pits of Tartarus. Have a nice trip! See you never!"

"I'm correct," Monty said. "The third cross is a direct reference to the Matthew 10:39 verse, the second thief. Losing your life to discover it, retaining it, to lose it. Don't you see? It makes perfect sense?"

"That seems thin," I said with a nod as my vision began to swim from the pressure. "But we've risked more on less."

I placed the obol in the mouth of the skull that formedced the center of the door with three crosses. For a few seconds, nothing happened, then the runes of the door shifted from violet to white.

The door slid to the side and all I could see was a wall of white.

A moment later, the wall of white began pouring into the Moon Hall, filling the space with a light fog.

"This would be a great door to have around Halloween," I said, looking at the fog filling the room. "Other than fog, it's not doing much—"

I began to notice that the fog was no longer escaping out of the door, but being sucked into it.

"It seems to be reversing direction," Monty said, looking around. "Did you actually place the obol in the skull's mouth?"

"No," I mocked. "I palmed it and put it in my pocket—of course I put the obol in the skull's mouth. Where else was I going to put it?"

"I don't understand," Monty said, looking around the empty room. "What went wrong?"

We came to the same realization at the same time.

There was nothing to hold onto in the empty room. The doors were all smooth and handle-less. The suction from the open door increased.

"Monty?" I said. "That pull is starting to get stronger."

Monty gestured and his symbols fizzled out before he could create anything.

"It appears we are now standing in a null zone," Monty said, looking at the tips of his fingers. "An exceptionally powerful null zone."

The suction increased and pulled us into the wall of white fog.

SIXTEEN

When I opened my eyes, everything was still white fog.

I lay on something soft, but it wasn't a bed or mattress. When I put my hand on the surface under me, it felt like wet grass only slightly more solid. I could make out some shapes in the fog, but nothing was sharp or clear.

It reminded me of my latest trip to London where rain and fog were the default setting for what passed as weather in that city.

"Monty?" I called out, slowly getting to one knee. "Peaches?"

My voice sounded flat, the acoustics of the area dulling the sound.

<Can you hear me, boy?>

A large, wet sock slapped me across the face, taking me by surprise.

"Agh," I managed before I was assaulted again. "What?"

That first wet sock was followed by another, and one more, before I managed to locate my hellhound's enormous head, push it to one side, and dodge the last tongue slap.

Slowly the fog began to lift.

Considering the absence of darkness, I figured there was a good chance we were *not* in Tartarus. That led me to the next question: where exactly were we?

<*I can hear you. Do you feel better now?*>

<*I was feeling fine before you tried to drown me in your saliva.*>

<*My saliva just healed you. I healed the angry man too. He wasn't too happy after that, but I know he is feeling better. Do you think he can make me some meat?*>

That visual brought a smile to my face.

<*Did you make sure he was completely healed?*>

<*Completely. I smacked him more times than I smacked you.*>

My smile grew wider.

<*I think we better wait a bit before asking him to make you some meat.*>

I knew that somewhere in this fog was an angry, soggy, mage, upset that his bespoke mageiform was covered in hellhound drool at this very moment.

What was he wearing this time?

"This is a Zegna!" Monty's raised voice sliced through the fog clear as crystal. "A bespoke, runed Zegna, with runes specially designed by Gildo himself!"

"That sounds very mage froufrou and upscale," I said, still not seeing him, but hearing his huffs as he made his way to my location. "How do those bespoke mageiforms handle hellhound drool? Does it stain?"

"This is not remotely humorous."

"Well, no," I said, trying to keep a straight face. "Not remotely, but up close and in your face, it's hilarious."

He broke through the fog and I lost it again.

Peaches had managed to miss most of his suit except for the shoulders—those were soaked—but that wasn't where my hellhound unleashed his best work. It seemed that Peaches felt that Monty needed some kind of hairstyle makeover.

I took a moment, caught my breath and composed myself.

Monty's hair defied explanation. Peaches had hit it with so much drool that it was slicked back, doing its best Don Corleone impression.

"That's some...some look," I said, barely holding it together. "Is that the new mage hairstyle, Godfather Deluxe?"

I started coughing to cover the laughing. Actually, the laughing was making me cough.

"I'm so glad you find this humorous," Monty said. "You need to train your creature. This behavior is unacceptable."

"If you don't want him to give you new hairstyles," I managed between a few short gasps, "maybe you should make him an offer he can't refuse?"

"You are incorrigible," he glared at me, then glanced at Peaches. "Both of you are."

I glanced over at my sheepish-looking hellhound.

"I don't know if he needs anymore training," I said. "That hair style is making you look fabulous."

"Hellhound drool is *not* part of my grooming regimen," he snapped. "Tell him to keep his drool to himself."

"His drool heals, you know."

"I am not ill or harmed, thank you."

"See? It works."

He glared at me again.

With a gesture, he created a small whirlwind of rain and heated air around his body, washing his hair and drying his suit back to pre-drool status. He took a moment to look around and shot me another glare before ignoring me and heading off.

"Where are we?" I asked as I went after him, my hellhound trailing silently next to me. "I'm guessing this is not Tartarus?"

"You guess correctly," Monty said as we climbed up a small

set of hills. "This is the island of the Spartan, the home of the Hidden Hand. This is Naxos."

We paused a moment to take in the view.

It was incredible.

We looked over the bluest sea I had ever seen as the fog parted and allowed a view of the rest of the small island. The sun shone overhead and made the blue of the ocean appear even deeper. A soft breeze blew across the hill we stood on and smelled of the ocean.

The bluest sky descended to greet the ocean as I looked around in every direction. We were the only visible land mass for as far as I could see.

"Are you sure we're not on our plane?" I asked "This place smells like home."

"I can assure you, you are not home," a voice said from behind us. "Welcome to Naxos."

We both turned with our guards up—my hand reflexively dropped to Grim Whisper as Monty extended his arms to his sides.

We looked into the face of what I assumed, was the Spartan.

He was taller than Monty, thin, but wiry. His frame gave off the impression of holding a reservoir of kinetic energy, like a compressed spring under tension.

His energy signature was beyond impressive. I had a feeling he was revealing it for our benefit, since I hadn't sensed him approach us.

What he revealed made me reconsider using any type of weapon against him. I slowly moved my hand away from Grim Whisper.

He was way past our league.

I took a step back and *really* looked at him.

His bald head reflected some of the sunlight, and his gray robe fluttered in the wind, as he approached us.

"Tristan Montague and Simon Strong," he said, in a deep bass voice. I expected him to call me to the dark side in an amazing James Earl Jones impression. "I've been expecting you."

"You know who we are?"

"I do," he said. "You would be surprised at how many beings know who you two, or should I say three, are."

I held up a hand.

"Can you say: I am your father?"

"Simon," Monty hissed, glaring at me before turning to the Spartan. "My deepest apologies, Spartan."

The Spartan looked at me for a few seconds, then broke into a wide smile followed by a chuckle.

"I like you, Strong," he said. "I can understand your fear. But you must not succumb to it, despite the Emissary looking to end your life."

"That's one way not to get me to think about the murderous Emissary after us," I replied, giving him a look. "I see you went to the usual mage morale building seminar."

Monty shook his head.

The Spartan waved a hand in our direction.

"No apologies needed," he said. "Please call me H. I'm used to it after all these years. Spartan feels like I should be blocking the pass to Thermopylae."

"Were you there?" I asked. "You were part of the 300?"

"It was closer to several thousand, and I was...in the neighborhood at the time," he said. "But you're not here to discuss ancient history, are you?"

"I'm afraid we've brought death to your door," Monty said. "That Emissary in pursuit serves the Grand Council. She will be here soon."

"Not soon," H said and waved a hand across the ocean. "That should secure us enough time. It may be time to hold the Grand Council accountable for their actions."

The island rumbled as a tremor raced across the ground. I saw several waves rush out to the ocean as the edge of the island flared with violet light.

"What was that?" I asked, looking around the island. "What did you do? Is the island sinking?"

Peaches rumbled next to me.

"He shifted the island," Monty said, looking at H. "How?"

"Not the island," H answered. "Just the door to the Passage that leads to the island."

"You shifted the door?" Monty asked. "I didn't think it *could* be shifted."

"Give me a lever long enough and a fulcrum on which to place it, and I shall move the world," H said, paraphrasing Archimedes with a small smile. "Anything can be shifted, when you know how."

"That door was secured with a trinary lock," Monty said. "You managed to shift them as well?"

"Yes, and you only engaged two of them," H said. "A clever maneuver, but your Emissary will figure it out soon enough. By moving the door, I've bought us some more time." He glanced at me. "Maybe just enough."

"How can she even follow us?" I asked. "She doesn't meet all the criteria. Does she?"

"Good question," H said, turning and heading down the hill. "I'm afraid *you two* let her in. Come with me."

"We what?" I asked, following him down the hill. "How did we let her in? What was all that with walking with Hades and the obol? Are you telling me that was all a lie?"

"Simon," Monty said next to me, keeping his voice low. "Temper your voice. Remember who you are speaking to."

"Sorry," I said, raising a hand in surrender. "No disrespect meant."

"None taken," H said as he kept walking. "We will discuss the matter further, once we reach my home. It's just over the next hill." He glanced at me. "It should be adequate for what I need to share with you."

We crested the next hill.

The sight of H's 'home' froze me in place.

Even Monty was at a loss for words as we gazed down at what H called his *home*. I was a expecting a small home, something modest where one person could live comfortably.

I should know better than to have expectations.

H lived in a castle.

An enormous medieval, straight out of the history books, castle made of subtly glowing dark bricks. I didn't see any runes from where we stood, but I could feel the power emanating from the structure.

"That's one powerful castle."

"Yes," H agreed. "It contains some powerful runes. I inscribed them myself."

Monty narrowed his eyes as he looked at H's home.

"That's...that's Dover Castle?" Monty managed once he caught his breath. "How did you—?"

"You recognize it?" H asked. "I take it the original still stands, then?"

"It's only one of the most famous castles in the world," Monty said, still mildly shocked. "Yes, it stands still."

"That's comforting to hear. I helped design the original and realized it made a nice solid home," H said, looking down at the castle. "I decided to replicate it here with some modifications, of course. Welcome to Fenix, the Rising Talon."

"I don't remember any castles made of black brick on our last visit to England," I said under my breath to Monty. "Not that I'm a castle expert, but are you sure that's Dover Castle? It doesn't match any of the pictures I've seen."

"Not *the* Dover Castle, but the design is identical," Monty said as we approached a path that led to the castle. "This structure is considerably more runically enhanced."

"Fenix is more of a stronghold than the original," H said. "I have acquired a sizable number of enemies over the years; this place was constructed to keep them at bay."

"Emissaries are strong," I said, still looking at the castle. "I don't know if your stronghold is going to be strong enough. The last Emissary we faced was handling us without so much as breaking a sweat."

"I think we will be able to hold off an Emissary long enough," H answered, while giving me another strange look. "At least long enough to set you on the path."

"Set me on the path?" I asked "The path to where?"

"The path to where you need to be," H said. "We will discuss matters further once we are inside Fenix."

He gave me the usual mage non-answer as he directed us to step on a clearly designated path leading down the hill to Fenix.

I shook my head and followed him down.

SEVENTEEN

"Exactly how big is this island?" I asked, scanning the horizon as I paused on the path down the hill to take in the size of the island. "It didn't seem *this* large when we got here."

"Naxos is considered an unfixed loci," H answered as we walked down the path to the castle. "It contains expressions of time and relative dimensions in space. Certain parts of it will appear much larger from one perspective than others. Do we stay on the path."

"What happens if we step off the path?"

"Nothing at first," H said as he slowed his steps. "At least not until you get to that marker over there." He pointed to a tall, stone obelisk that stood near the entrance of the castle. "As an unfixed loci, Naxos doesn't react to certain events in real time."

"What happens when we reach that marker?"

"That is when the first temporal incongruity would become apparent," H said. "After a few minutes you would realize something was wrong."

"I don't follow," I said. "What temporal incongruity?"

"If anyone attempted to approach Fenix by any method

other than this path, they would be out of sync with Fenix," he said. "They would reach it eventually, but they would lag." He must have seen the look of confusion on my face. "When you were a young boy did you ever watch those excellent kung fu movies with the English dubbing?"

I nodded.

"Those were the best, especially the sound effects."

"When they spoke, you heard the words but the mouths would move completely out of sync with what they were actually saying, do you remember that?"

"I do," I said. "We would imitate that, too."

"I'm sure," H said with a nod. "Whoever attempts to cross that marker without being on the path or knowing the crossing sequence, would enter a similar state. They would be out of sync."

"It's castle defense," Monty said, looking down at the path. "What is the time gap?"

"Ten seconds," H said. "Once they cross that marker, if they are out of sync, anything they do won't actually occur inside Fenix for ten seconds."

"A ten second lag?" I said. "That's a lifetime in a fight."

H nodded.

"It gives the defenders a distinct advantage," he said. "You could attack or flee depending on who and what you were facing."

"Is there any way to counter something like that?" I asked. "I ask because...Emissary?"

"It's a wise concern," H said as we approached the stone obelisk. "Without knowing the specific sequence, it would require the total destruction of the obelisk."

He placed his hand on different sections of the obelisk, which lit up with a soft orange glow as he touched them. The obelisk thrummed with power as he activated the sequence.

"This doesn't feel that easy to destroy," I said, raising a hand and stepping closer to the marker. "Can I touch it?"

"Yes, avoid the runed sections."

The power vibrated under my hand as I lightly placed my palm against the smooth stone of the obelisk. It felt cool to the touch with an undercurrent of heat. To destroy this marker felt impossible. It contained more power than I could wrap my brain around.

"It's rooted to the island's core," Monty said, without touching it. "Is it even possible to destroy this marker?"

"Yes," H said. "All it takes is power. However, the power that would require...well, if this Emissary can do that, then you have greater problems to be concerned about if she is capable of its destruction. I only know one person capable of destroying this obelisk."

"What happens if its destroyed?"

"Naxos becomes unmoored," H answered. "It seals itself and drifts through time inaccessible to anyone. This obelisk is the only anchor keeping it fixed in this place and time."

"Essentially the entire island becomes a prison?" Monty asked, examining the obelisk. "A closed environment and pocket dimension?"

"Yes," H said. "It was designed that way in case any of the more volatile artifacts became too dangerous and needed containment."

The path shifted beneath our feet, widening and continuing past the marker.

"Do you think she can do it?" I asked, looking at Monty. "I mean if she's as strong as Alain, can she do it?"

"No," Monty said, shaking his head. "I have a feeling the Grand Council won't send someone *as* strong as Alain. From my understanding, Salya is considerably *stronger* than Alain."

"I had a feeling you were going to say that," I said, looking ahead as the path kept forming in front of us. I looked around the interior of the wall. Several small buildings sat around a large tower in the center. "A place like this must have several layers of defense, right?"

"She may be stronger, but I doubt she is strong enough to destroy *that* marker," he said, scanning the buildings inside the wall. "I only recognize the Great Tower; some of these other structures are unfamiliar. You dwell here alone?"

"Currently, I am alone," H said. "For those who can find it, Naxos is a special learning center. We have an extensive magical library and an artifact vault on the grounds. A small group of mages lives here as staff for several months at a time to help maintain the grounds."

"If Naxos is an unfixed loci, what is its relation to time?" Monty asked. "Does it correspond to the time on our plane?"

"A good question," H answered as we moved forward on the path and headed to the Great Tower. "Time flows slowly here, if it flows at all."

"Time doesn't flow here?" I asked. "This is a stasis area?"

"Not exactly," H said. "Let's just say time flows differently on Naxos."

"Is there a ratio?" Monty asked. "One that could place the flow into perspective, how time here compares to time on our plane?"

H paused and gave the question some thought.

I became a little concerned.

The last thing I wanted was to be stuck on this island, where one hour was similar to a year on our plane. It would not be good to get back home and find the city a ruin because we were on Naxos too long.

I'd call that a bad day.

"Not in the short term," H said after giving it thought. "In the short term, time can be non-linear inside Fenix. In the long-term, it works itself out to something like one day here being equal to ten minutes on your plane, I think."

"You think?" I asked. "You're not certain?"

"Time is not certain," H said with a reassuring smile, leaving me anything but reassured. "In any case, we have to get you started. Time is of the essence."

He pushed open the large doors of the Great Tower and stepped inside, leaving Monty, Peaches, and me just outside the entrance.

"Time is of the essence, after giving us that answer?" I asked. "Is he okay? He seems a little...you know, out of touch."

"Prolonged life—in this case, extreme prolonged life—can have deleterious effects on the mind," Monty said as we stepped inside. "He is not a god, merely a mage who mastered life-force manipulation. His mind may have suffered some negative side effects from his advanced age."

"Are you saying he has dementia?"

"No, but his relationship to reality, any reality, may be a loosely held association," Monty said, scanning the interior of the room. "I think he views life and the events of history through a distinctly different lens than we do."

The room was fairly large and sparsely furnished with some chairs, and a large lounge sat against one of the walls. An intricately designed rug dominated the center of the floor. Along the walls, I noticed banners which held a coat of arms, centered around a phoenix holding blazing swords. Behind the phoenix was a large sun and a field of peonies.

On some of the banners, instead of a phoenix, I saw a roaring dragon unleashing a stream of flame. One banner, the one farthest from the entrance and largest in the room, had both a phoenix and a dragon interlocked with each other, holding a blazing sword.

I was sure there was some meaning there, but I wasn't an expert on insignias or coats of arms. It did make sense that a castle named Fenix the Rising Talon would have the creature on banners all over the place.

"I can see that," I said, stepping in next to Monty after examining the banners hanging around the room. "You live long enough, I would imagine most things lose their meaning. Time takes away your friends, enemies, family, everyone eventually. You live to see empires and civilizations rise and fall, over and over. It must take a toll."

"It does," H said from a hidden staircase in the far wall. "Eventually you long for death, knowing it to be a futile desire. One that will remain unfulfilled. I fear it's a desire you are destined to experience, Marked One. It will happen one day, but not today."

"You know?"

"Your mark is apparent to one my age," H said. "Come now, we must begin your preparation immediately. Follow me and we will begin. Do not tarry."

He disappeared down the stairs.

"You think he heard us?" I asked as Monty headed for the stairs. "It's not like we were being subtle."

"We said nothing offensive," Monty said. "I'm certain he has heard it all before. Did Kali give you any indication as to what he was to instruct you in?"

"You expect Kali to give me, *me*, details?" I asked as we took the circular stairs down. "I'm surprised she tells me anything, really."

"True, she's not very forthcoming with you," Monty said. "This is probably due to your defense mechanism. How she hasn't blasted you to dust before now is truly a mystery to me."

"Me too," I said. "Maybe she really likes me?"

"I suppose that's a possibility," he said. "Or she plays a very long game. She is a goddess after all...she can wait."

"That's what I'm afraid of," I said. "I don't want to end up bitter and insane at the end of my days. H seems to be doing okay."

"We can only see the face he shows us," Monty said as we reached the bottom of the stairs. "However if it ever comes to that, I'm sure if you have a prolonged conversation with Kali, you can quickly get her to reverse your curse and blast you out of existence."

"Oh, mage humor, how droll," I said with a horrible fake English accent. "I'm beside myself with glee. I can barely contain the hilarity. Whatever will I do?"

"I do *not* sound like that," he said as he left the staircase and stepped into a sizable training area. Monty paused as he took the space in. "A mage training hall? This is an authentic representation dating back centuries."

"I feel it's important to keep to the old ways," H said from the center of a large circle on the other side of the room. He gave us both a look and stared a little longer at me. "Yes, I heard what you said. Please step into the circle, Strong."

"No offense intended," I said. "I was just a little concerned the cake may have been left in the oven a little too long and may have been over baked."

"Is that a euphemism for my going insane?"

"Something like that," I said. "I know what I'm risking by doing this, but what do you get for it? I'm sure you get something out of helping me, don't you?"

"I can assure you I'm not insane, at least not yet," H said. "Your words weren't offensive or anything I haven't heard countless times before. At my age, it's hard to find anything offensive."

"That's good to know," I said, approaching the circle. "You didn't mention what you get out of helping me."

"I get resolution," he said with a nod. "Please enter the circle."

"And my hellhound?"

"Will have to wait outside, along with Tristan," he said, staring hard at me before glancing at Monty. "No matter what you see in this circle, do not attempt to interfere. Your efforts will be futile and will hinder Simon's progress."

"What exactly do you intend to impart to him?" Monty asked. A good question, actually since I was getting serious 'run the other way' vibes from H right about now. "Which teaching?"

"One that existed before the name Montague ever existed," H said as he extended an arm to me. "Your concern, while touching, is unwarranted. I have a vested interest in this teaching succeeding."

"Why?" Monty asked, taking a step forward. "What is your interest?"

I stopped approaching the circle.

"My interest?" H asked, then shot his other hand forward in my direction. I felt myself dragged into the circle as a wall of energy shot up behind me. "My interest is death."

EIGHTEEN

I tried to remain calm.

I was trapped in a magic circle with an ancient mage who had gone from appearing sane, to dancing on the edge of madness in a heartbeat.

The wall of energy around the edge of the circle flowed slowly upward into the ceiling. It was semi-transparent and flowed with streaks of violet and gold. Outside of the circle, I could see Monty form an orb and release it.

It bounced off the wall of energy and disappeared.

I saw Peaches blink out and reappear as he slammed into the energy wall and bounced off, cratering the stone floor as he landed a few feet away.

"They will realize the futility of their actions soon enough," H said. "I apologize for my methods; I have waited a long time for this."

"What exactly is *this*?" I asked warily, keeping to the edge of the circle without actually touching the energy wall. "What have you been waiting for?"

"I told you—resolution," he said, gesturing and bringing

the symbols inside the circle to life. "You will give me resolution, and I will give you the inception to mastery."

"I don't understand," I said, doing my best to keep away from him. "Why don't you bring this wall down and we can have a civilized non-confined chat about this resolution?"

"I'm afraid I can't do that," he said. "I gave my word and accepted the conditions."

"Gave your word to who? What conditions? No one discussed conditions with me."

"I know, and for that you have my deepest apologies," he said, gesturing again and turning the green symbols in the circle a bright white. "You should have been consulted, or at the very least, informed."

"I agree," I said, drawing Grim Whisper. "How about we pause whatever it is you're doing, and discuss this, before I shoot you?"

"This circle is a transference circle," he continued as if I hadn't just threatened to shoot him. He closed his eyes and sighed. "Finally."

"Stop this, now," I said, aiming at his chest. "You seem like an okay guy for a demented immortal. I don't want to shoot you."

He gestured again and Grim Whisper disappeared from my hand and reappeared outside the circle next to Monty.

"How the—?"

"You won't need your weapons," he said, gesturing again, "any of them."

I felt a tugging sensation in my body, followed by a silver mist streaming from my chest. It flowed past the energy wall, coalescing next to Monty until it formed Ebonsoul. It hovered in the air next to him as I looked on in surprise.

"You extracted Ebonsoul?" I said, getting angry. "I warned you and tried to do this without violence. You didn't listen."

"No, I didn't, nor do I intend to."

"Your funeral," I said, gathering energy around me. "You should have listened. *Mors Ignis*."

I formed darkflame around both my hands.

Right away I knew something was wrong.

It could've been the fact that I sensed no fear from H. Or it could've been the slight smile he gave me when I formed the darkflame, as if he were expecting me to tap into my lifeforce.

Most likely it was the fact that he opened a hand and formed darkflame that engulfed not only his hand, but his entire body. His darkflame was black tinged with blue and raced across the floor filling in the symbols in the circle.

It was slowly making its way across the circle to where I stood.

I glanced at Monty who was gesturing furiously. Peaches was firing baleful glare beams at the energy wall when he wasn't trying to shred it with his fangs.

Nothing was getting past the energy wall H had created.

"You are fortunate to have such companions," H said as his flames got closer to where I stood. "You've tapped into darkflame, good. That will make this easier. I apologize for any pain or discomfort you will experience."

"So do I," I said and unleashed a blast of my darkflame at him.

My darkflame raced at him.

He extended a hand and caught the stream of my darkflame, absorbing it into his body.

He nodded and released more of his flame into the circle with his other hand as he snuffed out my flame, closing his hand into a fist.

"This will be the seed, the beginning of your awakening," he said as he poured more of his flame into the circle. I was running out of space in a hurry. "As you grow, more of this power will unlock. Remember that the key is in your mark; allow the flame to burn away your fear, and you will become stronger than any of your enemies."

"Right now I'm not in the mood for any kind of burning," I said, keeping an eye on the approaching flames. "How about we discuss this?"

"Your Emissary draws near," he said. "You, we, don't have time to discuss what I am giving you, but trust me, it will be revealed in time."

"Having a hard time on the trusting you front, right about now."

"It cannot be helped," he said. "Unfortunately, it must be this way. Perhaps one day, many years from now, if you are still alive, it will be explained to you."

"I get that more times than I want."

The flames were getting close enough to make my life considerably warmer. Sweat formed on my brow and was pouring into my eyes, forcing me to wipe it away with a sleeve.

I looked past the energy wall and saw Monty unleash a nasty black and red orb into the edge of the circle. It crashed into the wall and exploded with a burst of black energy, darkening the entire room.

When the energy cleared, the circle was still enclosed and Monty looked pissed. I didn't even want to guess what he had just tried to unleash.

H didn't even look in Monty's direction as he unleashed even more flames into the circle.

"Normally, your chances of survival would be low," H said, glancing at me. "But you've been cursed alive and that is what will make this transference possible. Brace yourself."

The flames were right by my feet. I looked down for a

brief second and then looked across the circle at H. He stared at me and nodded.

The flames that were at my feet, raced up my body and covered me completely.

For a brief moment, I felt nothing.

Then my world burned.

NINETEEN

The blue-black flame became a part of me.

As much as I shook or rolled, nothing put it out. The flames burned into me without burning my skin away. For a second, I looked down at my hands, which were on fire.

The flames burned hotter as searing pain overwhelmed my mind. I fell to my knees, covered in flames, and screamed. I screamed until I lost the ability to make any noise, and still the flames burned.

I fell on my side, the tears flowing freely and just as quickly being devoured by the intensity of the flames. I sensed H draw near and I tried to recoil, but I couldn't move. The pain had locked me into a fetal position and all I could do was wish for the end.

He placed a finger on my forehead and gestured with his other hand. A spike of power flowed from his finger into my forehead, threatening to split my head in half as a beam of white light shot out from my forehead.

He quickly placed his palm over the beam, covering my face, whispered something in a language I couldn't understand, and blasted me with a wave of golden energy.

"Now," he said quickly under his breath. "You're ready, now."

He pointed to the top of my head, my forehead, my throat, center of my chest, solar plexus, my abdomen, and my groin area. Each place he pointed to lit up with golden light.

"What...what are you doing?" I rasped. "Stop, please."

"I cannot," he said. "What has begun must be completed. Only a little longer, Strong. The pain will subside, but first you must be aligned."

"Just...just end me," I said through clenched teeth as another wave of pain wracked my body, forcing me to contract all my muscles. "This...this is...it's too much."

"Endure," he said. "You will endure because you must."

He placed a hand on my chest and the flames that were surrounding my body focused on one point in the center of my chest. A golden line of energy ran down the length of my body as my body still burned.

He placed another finger on my forehead and the golden line traveled up the center of my body and disappeared into my forehead, followed closely by the blue-black darkflame.

The agony raced into my body, burning everything inside of me.

"A little more," he said under his breath. "You're almost there."

I wanted to claw my chest open and let the energy out of me. I think I actually attempted to rip my chest open, because he gestured and my arms were forced to my sides.

"The final act of the transference," he said, placing a hand on my chest. "The Hidden Hand is now yours, Simon Strong, to be revealed to you as you grow in strength and knowledge. May it serve you as it served me. May you grow in wisdom all the days of your life."

He screamed something I didn't understand, and more golden light erupted from his hand and blasted into me. If it had been painless, I could have taken a moment to admire the power that he was unleashing.

I wasn't that lucky.

The pain rushed in right after the golden light appeared. I heard my bones break, followed by the tearing sensation of my muscles, ligaments, and tendons being torn to shreds.

I tried to scream again, but couldn't

My body exploded in heat as my curse repaired the damage. I lost vision in one eye, as I tried to look around to signal to Monty or Peaches that I was on my way out.

The pain was too much.

I turned my head to see where they were when a wall of black energy slammed into me, obliterating everything.

I floated in a deep darkness.

The pain was gone.

Am I dead?

Not yet, you aren't.

The voice was familiar.

Kali?

Yes and no.

How can that be if I'm not dead?

You tell me, my Marked One.

The realization rushed over me.

The mark, this is the part of you that is my mark?

A part of me which is always in and with you, yes.

How am I speaking with you?

You are aligned. The Spartan planted the seed in fertile ground. It will grow over time, as will you. He has given you the Hidden Hand.

What did you give him in return for this? What is his resolution?

You will see it with your own eyes in time. For now, you must prepare, death approaches.

I opened my eyes with a start and found myself still in the middle of the circle. The wall of energy was gone, as was H. Peaches lay on the ground next to me and Monty was seated in a chair a few feet away, still holding Grim Whisper and Ebonsoul in his hands.

I made to move and my entire body screamed at me. I realized I was on a thin, but insanely comfortable mattress that my sprawltastic hellhound was in the process of conquering by shoving me off of it.

I groaned as I shifted to one side.

"Good to have you back," Monty said as Peaches stirred and attempted to tongue-lash me. I placed a hand under his jaw and shut his enormous mouth before he could droolify me. "I heard his saliva has recuperative powers. Perhaps you should let him bathe you with his drool?"

"Pass," I said, slowly sitting up with Monty's help. "How can this thin mattress be so comfortable?"

Monty nodded.

"It's a battlefield mattress used by mages," Monty answered, looking at the thin mattress. "I haven't seen one of those in many years."

"What happened?" I asked. "I mean besides the agony. *That* I remember clearly."

"From what H explained, I'm not quite sure," he said. "You'll want these back." He handed me Ebonsoul and Grim Whisper. "Apparently, he planted a seed of knowledge within you, along with the Hidden Hand."

A brief recollection of the memory of H placing the Hidden Hand in me flashed before my eyes. I shuddered at the memory.

"He did what?" I asked. "I thought the Hidden Hand was a *person?*"

"I had no idea the Hidden Hand was an ability," Monty said. "I, too, always thought it was an identity. Apparently, I was mistaken."

"What does this Hidden Hand do?" I asked. "Do you know?"

"I'm afraid not," he said. "H said everything you will need will be in this."

He reached into his jacket and pulled out a thin, black journal. The exterior of the journal was plain except for a golden H on the cover.

"What's this?" I asked, taking the journal from Monty. "The Hidden Hand manual?"

"I don't know," Monty said. "It's blank for me."

I opened the journal and saw that Monty was right—the pages were blank until I focused, then lettering began forming on each of the pages.

"It's not blank," I said, looking at the pages filled with lettering. "These pages have writing on them."

"You'll have to share what it says at another time," Monty said with some urgency in his voice. "The Emissary is on her way and according to H, she's not alone."

"When I was in the circle, what did you unleash?" I asked. "That last orb that was black and nasty looking?"

"You don't want to know," he said. "It doesn't matter, it didn't work. Your creature couldn't breach the circle either."

I dropped it because he sounded anxious about the Emissary heading our way. If we survived her visit, I would press him about it. That orb looked dangerous and dark.

"I noticed it only bounced off," I said. "It did look powerful."

"Not powerful enough," he answered. "H is much stronger than I anticipated."

"Are we talking Archmage levels?"

"At least, though I surmise he has lost some of his power in the transference of the Hidden Hand to you," Monty answered as we moved. "Still, his energy signature is quite impressive."

"I don't feel any different," I said. "Maybe it takes a while to kick in?"

"I would imagine unlocking that power will require extensive study," he said. "In the meantime we have an Emissary to deal with."

"She unlocked the door?" I asked, putting the journal in my jacket pocket as we walked. "How long was I out?"

Monty nodded.

"Hard to tell in this place," he said, handing me a pair of sunglasses. "It felt like close to thirty minutes, but I have no accurate method of telling the passage of time here."

"What about your uber expensive Patek—?"

He held up his wrist to show me his timepiece.

It had frozen at three thirty.

"Somehow I don't think it's three thirty. Is it broken?"

"I doubt it," he said, glancing at it with a small sigh. "It stopped some time ago. So much for expensive timepieces. It should start again once we leave this plane; right now, we have to go find H."

"What are these for?" I asked, looking down at the sunglasses he had handed me. "I mean, it's a nice pair, Zegna even, very stylish, but I don't think I need these."

"You do," he said. "At least until you get your eyes under control. Let's go. H is waiting for us."

TWENTY

We climbed the stairs and left the lower level.

"My eyes?" I said. "What's wrong with my eyes?"

"You know how you don't like attracting attention?"

"Yes," I said. "What does that have to do with my eyes?"

We were on the ground floor in the room with the coat of arms banners. In between some of the banners hung small mirrors. Monty pointed to the full length mirror beside the largest banner.

I walked over to the mirror and understood immediately why he gave me the sunglasses. This was even worse than when I borrowed my hellhound's baleful glare.

My eyes were pulsing a deep violet.

"Do you *see* what it has to do with your eyes, now?"

"I saw what you did there," I said, putting on the glasses. "How long will my eyes be like this? Is this permanent?"

"Too many questions and right now we don't have the answers," he said as we left the Great Tower. "I don't know. I have to assume you will find some way to control this expression of power, or it's going to make our lives...complicated."

"No kidding," I said, looking around outside. The inner courtyard felt charged with energy. "What is H doing?"

"He charged the defenses," Monty said as Peaches gave off a low rumble. "He said he would be by the outer courtyard, near the Lunatic's Passage."

"Where is that?"

"On the other side of the grounds," Monty said, pointing to the side. "Over there."

I looked and saw a large courtyard just inside the outermost wall. I hadn't noticed the courtyard when we walked on the path earlier, which was strange because it was immense.

"Was there a river here at some point?" I asked, pointing to another building in the distance. "I'm only asking because, is that a lighthouse?"

Monty looked to where I pointed and nodded.

"It appears that H replicated some of the details exactly," Monty answered. "That ancient Roman lighthouse does exist on our plane, not in this exact location, but I don't see the need for it here. No evidence of a river is apparent."

Beyond the courtyard was a wall of shimmering orange energy inside a large archway was a large archway.

"I don't remember seeing that wall of energy either," I said. "How did I miss that when we walked down the path?"

"That is the trinary door," Monty said, his voice tight. "If it's appearing here, it means Salya unlocked the locks."

"That's not good," I said. "Can't you just lock it again?"

"Doesn't quite work that way," he said as we reached the edge of the outer courtyard. "The locks have been undone."

"Undone?" I said, focusing on the archway. "As in—?"

"No longer in existence."

"Oh, do we have any other defenses?"

"Plenty of them," H said, materializing next to us. "They are currently passive, but will activate once your Emissary arrives."

I turned at his voice, startled.

He looked different, older. His face had more wrinkles and I noticed that he walked a little slower. His energy signature was still impressive, but something was slightly off. The transference had taken a toll on him.

"You look..."

"There is always a cost, Simon," H said. "Remember that. How do *you* feel?"

"Sore all over," I said. "Like I've gone twenty rounds with an angry Tyson in his prime."

H chuckled and nodded.

"Sounds about right," he said. "That will pass. Any sharp pain?"

"No," I said, shaking my head. "Aside from the agony of what I just went through."

"My apologies, there was no other way," H said. "Not every candidate survives a Hidden Hand transference. I was one of the fortunate ones. You of course, had a distinct advantage, Marked One."

"I want to say thank you, but I don't even know what I'm thanking you for," I said. "It feels important, but it also feels like you just made my life a hundred times worse."

"Correct on both counts," H said. "Try not to tap into any new power once the fighting starts. My defenses and I will keep the Emissary engaged; you two deal with thinning her minions. With any luck, we can stop her here."

"And if we can't?" I asked as I glanced at Monty. "Alain was insanely strong. She's going to be stronger."

"We have the stronghold defenses, me, and the three of you," H answered, letting his gaze drift over to the archway. "If it appears we will fail, you fall back to the obelisk and I will force them off the path."

"Will it knock her out of sync?"

"That is the plan," he said. "That will give us a slight advantage, one we can use to defeat her."

"Ten seconds is not very long against an Emissary," Monty said. "That window will only provide you with one opportunity at most."

"I only need one opportunity," H said. "Remember, Strong. Do not attempt to tap into any new power once we begin. Rely on your weapons and the casts you always use. Understood?"

"Understood," I said, not exactly understanding. "Why, exactly?"

"If you miscalculate the source of energy you could disintegrate yourself," he said, looking at me. "That would be bad. I don't know if your curse could bring you back from something that catastrophic. That's why."

"That's a good reason, actually."

"I'm glad you agree. Remember, I will engage the Emissary," he said. "Do not underestimate her minions. They may be weaker than her, but that does not make them weak. They pose a real threat. Treat them as such."

"Do we know how many are with her?" I asked. "I heard she likes to work alone."

"Consider that, even if it's one other, that person is accompanying one of the most dangerous Emissaries on an extermination operation," he said. "What does that tell you?"

"That we need to take whoever it is seriously."

"Precisely, now get ready," he said, stepping forward. "The doorway is becoming active."

I looked over to the archway as the orange energy inside began to swirl around. It became brighter with every passing second as the energy moved faster and faster. After a few seconds it turned black and figures began walking through.

The Emissary was the first one through.

She wore a suit similar to what Alain had worn when we

faced him, except hers must've been the battle version. Her suit looked like combat armor and was covered in golden defensive runes.

Her black hair was about shoulder length and held several runed silver barrettes. I doubted they were for decoration. I didn't see an actual main weapon, but I noticed the daggers on her arms and thighs.

She carried at least five runed daggers on each arm and leg.

She was a walking arsenal.

I didn't notice a spear or any blade larger than those nasty-looking daggers on her. It didn't mean she didn't have one, just that I couldn't see it at the moment. For all I knew, she could have it stored in some pocket dimension like Monty did with his crybabies.

Her dark eyes glistened with power as she moved forward, scanning the area as she stepped through the archway.

Behind her, two Magistrates stepped out, one to each side of her. Behind the Magistrates, several squads of Sanitizers ran out of the archway, filling the space behind them as they stepped forward.

She alone radiated 'I'm going to rip you apart' power. Everyone else that came through the archway after her was overkill. Even from this distance, her energy signature was oppressive.

In that moment, I realized why she worked alone.

She didn't need anyone else; she was an army of one.

H stepped forward, motioning for us to remain where we stood. His gray robe fluttered in the breeze as he walked toward the death squad. Clouds had formed, and the bright sunny day had become overcast.

Salya turned her gaze to the approaching H and smiled.

"Emissary Amrita," H said in a clear and powerful voice

that I knew he had enhanced somehow. "Welcome to Naxos. To what do I owe the honor of your presence?"

"Spartan," she said, her voice carrying just as clearly over the space between them. "Or should I call you the Hidden Hand? I'm here for Tristan Montague, Simon Strong and his hellhound. The Grand Council, by unanimous consent, has issued an edict declaring them outcasts, to be executed, in every sense of the word, immediately."

"H will suffice, Emissary," H said. "I'm afraid the Grand Council has no jurisdiction on Naxos."

The smile never left her face.

"The Grand Council exerts its jurisdiction wherever one of its agents exists," she answered. "Comply, and this insubordination will be overlooked. Defy the Grand Council, and you will share their fate. Step aside."

"I'm afraid that's not going to happen," H said, extending an arm and forming a black, rune-covered blade. "I'm going to have to ask you to leave now."

"How polite," Salya said. "You wield Sunder? I do look forward to facing it in combat. Do you know why they sent me? I mean, besides the fact that Alain failed where he should have succeeded?"

"The Grand Council is too scared to come face us themselves?" I answered from behind H. "So they sent you?"

"You must be Strong," she said, looking at me and cocking her head to one side. "No, they sent me, because, unlike Alain, I do not allow ego to cloud my reason. They sent me because I am inevitable and single-minded of purpose."

"Congratulations," I said. "They sent you because you have a strong work ethic? Hurray for you. What do you want —a gold star, a pat on the head?"

She narrowed her eyes at me and her smile diminished slightly. I half-expected Monty or H to say something about my answers, but I had a feeling they knew what I was doing.

At least Monty did.

It didn't matter how powerful the mage was, pushing their buttons was easy when you knew how.

I knew how.

I could feel Monty gathering energy next to me. Peaches had let out a low rumble as I let my hand drift closer to Grim Whisper.

The dying was going to start soon.

"I'm going to enjoy killing you, Strong," she answered, keeping her voice calm under her rage. "I wasn't going to make this personal, but I think, in your case, I could make an exception."

"Take a number," I said. "That line is long."

"The Grand Council sent me because I am the only Emissary that fills their hearts with dread," she continued, slowly unleashing her energy signature as she spoke. "They sent me because they fear me and hope you will do what they lack the spine to do. They sent me to kill you or die in the process."

Her energy signature washed over me, trying to fill me with fear. For a moment it worked; my only thoughts were of running back to the Great Tower behind me and hiding in the basement.

Then I heard *her*.

Kali.

My Marked One fears nothing, not even death.

I almost turned my head to see if she was next to me, her voice was that vivid and close. Then I remembered the mark. There was a part of Kali in and with me at all times. It was a strangely comforting and creepy thought.

"Nice try," I said, looking at the Magistrates and Sanitizers. "I thought you worked alone. Maybe the Grand Council doesn't think you're up to this job."

She laughed then and I had the feeling I may have pushed things too far over the edge of insanity.

"You think your insults can goad me into action?" she asked. "All my life I have heard worse, until the insults became the praise I craved. Over time, not even the insults could reach me." She looked to her sides and motioned to the squads around her. "Every single person you see beside me has been consigned to death by the Grand Council. Their presence here is the Grand Council's version of a divine wind. You should feel honored."

She let the words sink in.

The Magistrates and Sanitizers were on a suicide mission. They didn't expect to survive this trip to Naxos.

She smiled again as the realization set in.

"You understand now," she said with a nod. "Surrender, and I will make your deaths swift. Except you, Strong; I will make you suffer for your words."

"Don't I feel special," I said, backing up a few steps. "I'm going to decline your offer, thanks."

"It doesn't matter," she said. "I will be the only one leaving Naxos today."

TWENTY-ONE

Monty pulled one of his crybabies from behind him. The blade wailed as he swung it to his side and formed an orb with his other hand. The orb he formed was a mix of silver and gold and gleamed in his hand, nearly blinding me.

I had never seen him form an orb like that.

H ran forward and stopped suddenly as I drew Grim Whisper behind him. He extended an arm and stopped us from advancing.

In front of us, as Salya gestured, a surge of power filled the courtyard as the two Magistrates ran from Salya's sides. The Sanitizers around her weren't so lucky.

She reached back and produced a long, iron spear, proving my theory of a pocket dimension correct. It was easily six feet long and covered in angry red runes.

Just looking at it, I knew getting hit by that thing was a bad idea. All around her, Sanitizers dropped to the ground, dead before they hit the stone of the courtyard.

Salya began to laugh.

The Sanitizers that saw what was happening around her

decided that it was safer to try and kill us and ran in our direction. H raised his blade and the clouds in the overcast sky suddenly turned a darker gray.

From behind us, I heard a deafening roar. I glanced back and my brain seized for a moment. From the actual walls of Fenix, I saw large humanoid shapes step out. They looked vaguely familiar.

Golems.

Part of the defense of the castle was that the walls themselves which were made of golems. Flying high over us and raining fiery death on the Sanitizers, I saw what looked like small dragons covered in flames.

When I looked closer, I realized they weren't mini dragons, they were closer to mutant birds about twice the size of eagles, with extended tails. They used their tail feathers as flame whips as they attacked when they weren't unleashing spouts of flame at their targets.

Every so often, H would point and a bolt of black lightning would hit the ground, incinerating a Sanitizer where they stood.

H closed on Salya as Sanitizers headed my way. Behind the Sanitizers, I saw one of the Magistrates coming at me, his hands were covered in black energy. Things would end badly if I let him hit me with it.

I quickly scanned the battlefield and found the other Magistrate heading for Monty. There was no way he could help me; he would have his hands full dealing with a Magistrate, and H was headed for Salya and her Death Spear.

I was on my own.

Not entirely.

I felt my hellhound next to me.

<Battleform, boy? There's an angry-looking Magistrate coming this way with a group of Sanitizers looking to clean us up permanently.>

<YES, BONDMATE. IT IS TIME TO EMBRACE YOUR POWER. ENTER THE BATTLEFORM.>

I turned back and realized I had stepped into his flank. He turned his head and looked down at me.

My hellhound had gone XL

The last time he had entered a battleform, he was larger, but not this large. His fur had gone a deep blue-black with a metallic sheen.

The runes on his flanks blazed with red and violet energy and matched the runes which suddenly appeared on my arms. The part I could decipher read: *Bondmate* and then mentioned Cerberus and Hades. The rest was impossible to understand.

I would have to ask Hades about that, if I survived.

<Can you enter a battleform at this size?>

<OUR BATTLEFORM IS MEANT FOR ME TO BE AT THIS SIZE. I PREVIOUSLY DIMINISHED THE SIZE TO PREVENT HARM TO YOU. ONLY A FEW MORE LEVELS AND YOU WILL BE READY FOR THE FINAL FORM.>

I felt my skin become denser as one of the Sanitizers unleashed an orb at me. Peaches stepped in front of me and took the orb in the side with little effect.

<Thanks. Let me see if I can convince them that flinging orbs around is a bad idea.>

I fired Grim Whisper and managed to hit absolutely no one.

"I don't miss," I muttered, to myself, as I dodged another orb. "What is going on?"

<YOUR FIREARM WILL BE INEFFECTIVE IN THIS BATTLE. YOU MUST USE YOUR BLADE.>

I formed Ebonsoul as the Magistrate closed on us.

Peaches whirled his body around and sent three Sanitizers flying as his shoulder slammed into them. The Magistrate slashed in my direction. I backpedaled out of range as he fired a beam of black energy at me.

I reflexively threw up a hand, formed a violet wall of energy and deflected the beam into another Sanitizer, who screamed before crumpling to the ground.

I saw Peaches take a breath and braced myself behind my wall of energy. The Magistrate formed another orb. He was about to unleash it at me when my hellhound barked.

The wall I was taking cover behind disintegrated.

The ground rumbled as the sound wave tore through the courtyard, aimed at the Magistrate.

Too late, he realized he was the target.

Turning, he gestured with his other hand, trying to create some kind of shield.

It didn't work.

The half-formed shield was barked away and the Magistrate was launched away before he could release his orb, which exploded a second after he took flight. He landed hard on the far side of the courtyard as five more Sanitizers zeroed in on Peaches.

Monty was holding his own with the other Magistrate, but just barely. He didn't have an oversized hellhound to give him an assist.

I could change that.

<*Monty needs help!*>

<*I WILL OFFER THE MAGE ASSISTANCE AND RETURN. STAY SAFE, BONDMATE.*>

Peaches blinked out.

The five Sanitizers that were focused on my hellhound suddenly found a new target.

Me.

They attacked as one.

I parried the first thrust, and dodged the second, as the third Sanitizer tried to remove one of my legs below the knee. I switched leads and graced him with a kick to the face, knocking him out of the fight along with some teeth from his mouth.

One down, four to go.

"You don't want to do this," I said, moving back as they closed. "I'm warning you, I have a hellhound and I'm not afraid to use him."

"Your hellhound can't save you now," one of the Sanitizers answered with a sneer. "He's busy saving the mage, which means, you get to die."

"I'm not appreciating your tone," I said, as I parried a blade aimed for my midsection and backhanded a Sanitizer coming up behind me. Three more to go. My senses were on overdrive. I could sense everything and everyone around me. "Sneaking up on me? That was dirty."

One of the Sanitizers flung a black orb at me.

It wasn't as powerful as what the Magistrate had tried to hit me with, but it didn't feel friendly. I tracked the orb as I slid to the side.

The orb followed my motion, which was perfect.

At the last moment, right before it would hit me, I dodged behind another Sanitizer. The orb crashed into him and he fell to the ground, screaming.

That's when the anger rose.

"No more playing around," I said, under my breath. *"Ignis vitae."*

I outstretched my hand and a beam of violet-gold energy blasted from my palm. It caught the remaining two Sanitizers by surprise. If I was being honest, it caught me by surprise too.

The beam punched into them, launching them back to the castle wall behind us. Two of the golems stomped by and crushed them underfoot.

I heard Salya laughing as she engaged with H.

He was holding her off, but she was beyond skilled. Even if I could, I wouldn't know how to enter their fight. I was barely able to keep up with the attacks and parries. H was at least on her level, but he was slowing down and she looked like she was just getting started.

She extended an arm and fired a blast of red energy at a golem, exploding it into pebbles without missing a beat in her fight. She switched hands, swinging her Iron Spear in a semi-circle to her side.

Her spear blazed with a blue light as it cut through a group of Sanitizers, killing them instantly, and as it impacted another golem, reducing it to dust.

She managed this without taking her attention off H.

We were outclassed.

I knew it then as Monty, with Peaches' help, launched his Magistrate across the courtyard and into the outer wall which he hit with a sick crunch and fell lifeless to the ground.

The second Magistrate was coming my way again.

This time he wasn't going to take any chances. Around him whirled a small constellation of crackling black orbs. I took a quick scan of the battlefield.

Peaches was chomping on some Sanitizers and flinging them across the courtyard to the waiting golems, who proceeded to turn them into paste.

Monty had created a lattice and trapped a group of Sanitizers as a pair of phoenixes swooped down and flambéed them.

Their screams were short-lived.

The Magistrate that was coming my way had death in his eyes. I recalled H's words: *Do not attempt to tap into any new power once we begin.*

I looked down at Ebonsoul in my hand.

I was standing alone as I stared down the Magistrate.

My weapon and my wits were the only thing standing between me and a gruesome death at this Magistrate's hands.

I took off my sunglasses.

He paused when he saw my eyes.

It was only a moment, but that was all I needed.

I threw Ebonsoul at him and drew my gun as I yelled.

"Mors Ignis! Exuro!"

I fired Grim Whisper with one hand as I flung out the other, sending a beam of black energy at the Magistrate. There was no way he could avoid all three of my attacks at once.

His orbs came at me, but the black flame that escaped my hand intercepted them on its way to the Magistrate. He gestured furiously when he saw the orbs didn't reach me and managed to erect a shield.

He was fast and skilled.

It wasn't enough.

The black flame I unleashed was actually faster than the round I fired from Grim Whisper. The flame reached him first, destroying the shield. The entropy round punched into his chest a moment later, knocking him back as Ebonsoul buried itself in his abdomen.

I rushed over to remove Ebonsoul, but it was too late. I felt his power flood into me as he died. Ebonsoul became silver mist and flowed into my body.

That's when I felt it.

I felt the moment Ebonsoul, a necrotic blade, devoured and destroyed the Magistrate's soul.

"That is what he has become," I heard Salya say from across the courtyard as she tried to hit H with a downward strike. "That is why he must be stopped, here, today."

I turned to face her with sadness and anger in my heart.

"You want to stop me?" I asked, raising my voice as rage

flowed through me, filling me. "I'm right here. You want to kill me? You think you can?"

"I do," Salya said, releasing a barrage of energy spikes at H. He managed to deflect most of them, but several made it past his defenses, knocking him back to the nearby wall and impaling him against it. "Don't go anywhere, I'll be right back."

"Simon, no!" Monty yelled from a distance. "She *will* kill you!"

The Marked One fears nothing, not even death.

"She can try," I said with a voice that wasn't my own as I backed up and stood on the path. "Let's see if she has the guts to try."

H managed to remove himself from the wall with a grunt as he called down a bolt of black lightning at Salya. She looked up as the energy raced down at her and held up her spear.

The black energy flowed down her spear and into her body as she laughed. She turned to face H.

"You think this is a game?" she screamed, and raised her spear. "I am here to end you all!"

Black energy exploded from her spear, slammed into H, and engulfed the archway. The black energy in the center of the archway started swirling again.

That can't be good.

A few moments later, more figures began racing into the courtyard. More Sanitizers, more than I could count, were rushing through the archway. This could only end one way.

We were going to lose.

Peaches blinked in next to me at regular size. A few moments later, Monty, supporting a battered and bloody H, was next to me.

"Now where were we?" Salya said, as she turned back to

me. "Oh, yes, you were inviting me to your death. You're not having a change of heart, now, are you?"

"You can't beat her, not as you are now," H said, with a raspy voice. "Stay on the path and head to the obelisk, it's our only chance. Hurry!"

Salya smiled as we backed up on the path.

"Retreat? Really?" she asked, as she approached us. "Where is the bravado? I saw you undo my Magistrate, I *felt* what you did. You will become a monster. You've already begun. You will kill indiscriminately. No one will be safe from you or that cursed blade—no one."

"You're wrong," I shot back. "That was self-defense. Your Magistrate wanted to kill me."

"Where can you go that I cannot find you?" she asked. "Self-defense? No, Simon Strong, that was murder. I know it and deep down, in the darkest parts of your soul, you know it as well. Soon, that blade will control you."

"You're wrong," I said. "No one controls me."

The obelisk was behind us.

H leaned on it and turned to face Salya.

"This is your last opportunity to leave, Emissary," H warned. "Leave Naxos."

Salya stopped and looked around the courtyard.

Golems and Sanitizers were engaged in heated battle with the golems losing. Several of the phoenixes were shot down and their numbers were becoming fewer by the minute.

Over at the archway, I could see still more Sanitizers coming through the doorway. We were outnumbered and outclassed.

Salya turned back to H.

"I think I *will* take your advice," she said, tapping her spear on the ground next to her. "Right after I end *you*, old man."

She extended a finger, and a thin beam of black energy punched into H, hitting him in the center of his chest.

He gasped with surprise at the attack and leaned back on the obelisk.

"H!" I yelled, trying to prop him up. "Hold on."

Monty began to gesture and Salya raised her spear, pointing it at him. H grabbed Monty's hand and shook his head.

"No, you must not," H said.

"The one smart thing you've done today," Salya said, lowering her spear. "Futile, but wise."

She looked around.

"As final resting places go, this isn't too bad," she continued, then stared hard at me. "You're just full of surprises. A shame you have to die here. You could have made an excellent Magistrate."

"Emissary," H said, and pulled me close. "A final word."

"Who am I to deny a dying man his final words?" she asked, waving H's words away. "By all means."

"The circle where you endured is your only exit; where I end, you begin," he said with a wheeze. "That is my resolution."

"Cryptic nonsense as usual with these old mages," Salya said. "Time for your final rest, Spartan. You should have surrendered."

H placed his hand on certain sections of the obelisk as he slid down its side. He looked up at Salya and smiled.

"And you should have left when you could."

H extended a hand and Salya raised her spear in a defensive move as he turned to us. With a motion he shoved us back, off the path.

"Ten...ten seconds," he rasped, and gestured again. "Go, now!"

A field of energy formed around H and Salya, trapping them on the path with the obelisk.

"We're out of sync," Monty said. "We have ten seconds."

"But, H," I said, looking at him as he lay there smiling at a raging Salya who couldn't break the field around them. "He's stuck in there with her."

"Do not insult the gift he gave us," Monty said, running toward the Great Tower. I ran after him with Peaches by my side. We dashed inside and raced to the staircase. "Downstairs, quickly!"

TWENTY-TWO

We reached the lower level as the ground above us trembled.

The circle of transference activated with the symbols coming to life with green energy. A piercing scream reached us, followed by a deafening roar as the Great Tower shuddered and swayed, sending debris everywhere.

We stepped into the circle and Monty gestured. Peaches nudged even closer to my leg as I turned to look at the staircase. Salya was coming down the stairs when a large slab of the ceiling collapsed and blocked her path.

The last thing I saw was black energy erupting around the slab, shattering it to pieces, as Naxos disappeared from view in an explosion of green light.

We landed, painfully, in a different courtyard that I didn't immediately recognize, where I bounced across the stone floor and crashed into a column which didn't have the courtesy to move out of the way.

"What kind of teleport was that?" I asked, with a groan as the courtyard gently swayed around me. "You really...really need some practice."

I looked over to the side and saw Monty flat on his back,

looking about as bad as I felt. He raised a hand to his head and groaned in response. Only my hellhound looked like he enjoyed the trip.

"That could have gone better," he said. "We were lucky to get out when we did. Naxos completely sealed itself which resulted in our being shunted out of its space. One more second..."

"Let's not think about one more second," I said, laying on my back. "Do you think the Emissary—?"

"She's trapped, at least for now," Monty said, slowly getting to his feet. "She won't remain that way for long. I grossly underestimated her power. There's no way we can face her as we are now."

"Aye," a familiar voice said behind us. "We aim to correct that, right now."

Dex.

"Correct what how?" I asked, warily. "We just barely escaped Naxos."

"I see," Dex said, looking at me. "H?"

"He didn't make it," I said. "Salya took him out."

"Did you see him die?" Dex asked. "You saw his death?"

"I saw her hit him with a death beam," I said. "Right in the chest."

Dex smiled.

"You didn't see him die," Dex said. "H is almost as bad as Nana when it comes to this. I do see he passed the Hidden Hand to you. Did he manage to give you his journal?"

I patted my jacket and found the journal in an inside pocket, right next to my flask. I pulled it out and showed it to Dex who nodded.

"Good," he continued. "Congratulations. You're going to need that where you're going."

"Where *are* we going?"

"Iron Fan Mountain," Dex said. "Yat is waiting for you."

"What, now?"

"The one thing you do not have an abundance of, boy, is time," Dex said. "The Emissary is trapped, not dead. What do you think she will be doing her every waking moment?"

"Finding a way to get off Naxos," I said. "Can she?"

Dex nodded.

"Aye, which means you two need to get stronger in a hurry," Dex answered. "Only place to do that is on Iron Fan Mountain."

"Why does that sound like impending agony?"

"What's a little pain?" Dex said, with a gesture. "I promise to make the trip a smooth one. You need to access the power H gave you, and you"—he looked at Monty—"you need to accelerate a shift, at least one. Two would be better."

"Two shifts?" Monty said, incredulous. "Wouldn't doing it that quickly risk a schism?"

"Can't be helped, lad," Dex said, forming a large circle under us as Monty stepped close. "The Grand Council will step in once they discover their Emissary is trapped. She won't remain on Naxos long after that."

"Bloody hell," Monty said. "This truncated training will be brutal."

Dex smiled.

"I'll visit when I can," he said. "I need to keep the Grand Council off your scent for as long as possible. Make the most of the time while you're there. Ready?"

"Just for the record, this is not my idea of a vacation," I said, as I nodded. "Ready."

"You can rest when you're dead," Dex said, with another smile. "Although with your particular condition, that may be a bit difficult. For now, you have an Emissary to stop. Go get stronger."

He touched the edge of the circle and green light blinded me as Dex and the School of Battlemagic vanished.

TWENTY-THREE

IRON FAN MOUNTAIN
Tibet

We stood somewhere high up in the mountains.

"Where are we?" I asked. "Is this Tibet? It's freezing up here. I am not dressed for mountain weather."

"That mountain up there in the distance is Iron Fan Mountain," Monty said, pointing to a peak partially obscured by clouds. "That is our destination."

"Up there?" I asked. "Way up there?"

He nodded.

"Wow, I'm afraid I left my mountain climbing equipment back at the school," I said, shaking my head. "That's a real shame. I guess we'll have to postpone—"

Thwack!

A sharp pain bloomed on the side of my head.

"No mountain equipment needed," Master Yat said, as he stepped forward. "There are stairs. Many, many stairs."

"Wonderful," I said, rubbing the side of my head. "I don't

suppose there's a temple or training area at the base of the mountain?"

"The air at the *top* of the mountain is ideal for training," Yat answered. "I would not want you deprived of the best training environment. You have much to learn and little time to learn it. We must begin."

"Can we at least catch our breath?" I asked. "I mean, we just got here."

"Are you having difficulty breathing?" Yat asked. "Has your breath escaped you?"

"Well, no," I said. "It's a figure of speech. You know, it means take a moment to get our bearings?"

Monty shook his head.

"What?" I asked. "That's what it means."

"Ah, a moment to get your bearings?"

"Yes, you know, a moment to—"

A blow smashed into my solar plexus, forcing the air from my lungs and doubling me over. I wheezed as I tried to catch my breath, literally this time.

"And now?" Yat said, as he bent over to look me in the face. "Has your breath escaped you?"

"Yes...yes," I said, between gasps. "It escaped me."

"It has escaped you because you were not focused," he said. "If you are focused, you will always know where your breath is. What is the lesson, Strong?"

"I need to focus more."

"Good," Yat said, with a curt nod. "Now we can begin the climb to Iron Fan. As we climb, do your best to catch your breath."

He headed off up the path that lay before us. Above us, I noticed eagles soaring around the mountain peaks.

"Keep your wits about you," Monty said, as he walked next to me. "The path to the Stone Temple is not without its dangers."

"More dangerous than Master Yat?"

"Who do you think taught Master Yat?" Monty asked. "This place is where he learned to *be* Master Yat; do you really think it's safe for us?"

"When you put it that way, no," I said. "This is a frying pan and fire situation, isn't it?"

"We left the frying pan the moment we arrived here," Monty said. "Keep an eye out for the Elders."

"The Elders?"

"Not those Elders. These Elders wear red and white robes and walk around with a runed staff similar to Master Yat's. They're quiet and can strike you before you realize you're in striking distance."

"How many of these Elders are there?"

"I don't know," Monty said, as we followed Master Yat up the path. "I've never been able to get an accurate count. More than three, but less than one hundred is my best guess."

"Your best guess sucks," I said, looking around. "They're going to be out here on the mountain path? It's freezing out here."

"When you least expect them, expect them," Monty said. "Especially Sneak Attack Han. He is the most dangerous."

I chuckled at the name.

"Cmon, seriously? Sneak Attack Han?" I asked. "That's the name of an Elder, really?"

"Yes, and as I said, when you least expect an attack, expect one," Monty said. "Keep your senses wide and trust your innersight."

"You're serious?"

I felt Peaches pad silently next to me as we climbed the mountain. He nudged me in the leg and I rubbed his extra large head as we walked.

"Most certainly," Monty said. "Don't forget why we're here."

"I haven't," I said. "This is a crash course in Emissary stomping."

"Not the words I would use, but yes, we are here to grow stronger," Monty answered, with a nod. "The Iron Fan monks hold firm beliefs regarding growing stronger when it comes to mystic arts."

"Lots of scroll reading and sitting under waterfalls in meditation?" I asked. "Or is it a little more hands-on?"

"Much more hands-on than you will appreciate, trust me," Monty said. "Be on your guard, always."

I raised an eyebrow at him.

"We're out here in the middle of nowhere," I said, stretching out an arm at the vast amount of nothing around us. "You expect me to 'be on my guard' from some monk attack out here on a mountain? Then you tell me I'm the one who's been watching too many movies."

"You've been warned," Monty said, shaking his head and walking ahead. "Watch the pebbles."

"Watch the pebbles?" I repeated. "What's that even supposed to mean? Is that some zen—"

A pebble slammed into my temple.

"Ow!" I said, rubbing my head. "Very funny, Monty. Watch the pebbles, then you hit me with a pebble?"

"Wasn't me," he said, from where he stood. "I did warn you."

"You are not very aware for an Aspis," a voice said, next to me. "It would be child's play to neutralize you. Not much of a threat."

"Excuse me?" I said, turning in the direction of the voice. "Who are—?"

I looked around and saw an impossibly old man, wearing a red and white robe sitting on a large stone on the side of the path. In one hand he held a long runed staff similar, I noticed, to Master Yat's. I looked ahead and saw Master Yat in the distance. Behind him I saw Monty.

This wasn't some illusion.

At least I didn't think it was, not yet.

"You think too much," he said, and whacked my foot with his staff, hard enough to make it hurt. "Too much in your head."

I stepped back out of range.

"What's with the hitting?" I asked. "That doesn't seem very polite."

"What's with the lack of focus?" he replied. "How are you going to protect anyone, when you can't protect yourself? Can you sense anything beyond your nose?"

A pebble hit me in the back of the head.

I turned to see who threw it, but no one was there. When I turned back, the monk was gone. I rubbed my head as I kept walking.

"Can you sense anything beyond your nose?" I mocked. "Easy to say when you have monks ambushing me."

I caught up to Monty, still rubbing the back of my head.

"Sneak Attack Han?" Monty asked.

I nodded.

"Someone ambushed me when I was talking to a monk," I said. "Hit me from behind."

"Pebbles?"

"Are you sure this wasn't you?" I asked. "I wasn't a target until you started mentioning pebbles."

"I can assure you it wasn't me," he said, shifting his head to one side as another pebble smacked me in the face. "See? We're both targets."

"Ow," I said, rubbing my face. "So not funny."

"If I were you, I'd learn to dodge the pebbles as soon as possible," Monty said as we approached a large temple. "The projectiles get larger over time."

Master Yat was waiting for us at the entrance to the temple.

"Welcome to Stone Temple," Master Yat said, with a small bow. "Your training begins now."

THE END

Get exclusive short stories and new ebook releases for free:
https://www.patreon.com/bittenpeachespublishing

Keep reading! Three free novellas for you:
https://BookHip.com/PZWGAVV

AUTHOR NOTES

Thank you for reading this story and jumping into the world of Monty, Simon & Peaches with me.

Disclaimer:

The Author Notes are written at the very end of the writing process.

This section is not seen by the ART or my amazing Jeditor.

Any typos or errors following this disclaimer are mine and mine alone.

I know. I know. Most of you are breathing out a sigh of relief and saying...It's about time, actually it's WAY past time!

First, if you are reading this (kudos to you for being awesome!) I want to express my most sincere and humblest THANK YOU!

I know I do this in most of my books, but you have to appreciate the magnitude of what completing this book represents...this is book 25...BOOK 25!

25 books in the M&S series...that is incredible!

Okay, I've stopped hyperventilating.

Really (but not really).

I couldn't do this without you, my reader. I do appreciate you taking time out of your life to share with the creations of my imagination, and I hope you get a few hours of enjoyment and escape from the caffeine induced stories that explode from my brain.

Now, back to our regularly scheduled program.

Yes, it's about time Simon gets his act together!

It has been a longish process. I mentioned this in one of the MoB Kaffeeklatsches, that many readers chastised me by saying that he's been at this for years, but I say nay! Even though, its been years for us in real time, in M&S time has it really been that long?

Think back to the gaps between books, its not years between books, Monty & Strong get very few breaks lasting more than a few weeks, so I say Simon is doing pretty well for a mostly normal person thrust headfirst into the world of mages and the supernatural.

(That's my story and I'm sticking to it.)

In any case, its time he stepped up and owned up to his choices. If you're reading this I hope you're reading this AFTER reading the book. If not, go back and finish the book for mild spoilers lie ahead.

<giving you a MAJOR Clint Glint—go finish the story FIRST>

.

.

.

As I was saying, some mild spoilers ahead.

Simon has to own up to the choices he made in NO GOD IS SAFE. He has to accept that he's not entirely human any longer and what it means to be an immortal. In addition to all of this, he has to deal with the new caliber of enemies coming after him, Monty and Peaches.

His dawnward needs work, but he also needs to grow in

other aspects. This is the book where he makes that pivot and accepts it, because Salya, the Emissary the Grand Council sends after them is a serious threat in this and the next book.

She's a threat they can't face, at least not yet.

What does that mean?

<checks notes>

Send Earth destroying asteroid—it slams into planet, precipitating the end of the series.

<checks notes again, destroys *those* notes>

Sorry about that <cough>.

It means Simon & Monty need to get stronger and somehow evade enemies while they do this. It also means they need to become proactive. Instead of waiting or reacting to mages and beings trying to stomp them, now they have to go out and do some of the stomping first.

Remember, with the Grand Council: there are no rules, but they are going to wish there were, once Monty & Strong get started.

Let's discuss the ending to this story, no not THAT way, I'm not going to spoil it, but if I was being honest, it is a bit of a hillhugger. Yes, that's a word (I just made up) look it up, and if its not in your dictionary, your dictionary is seriously out of date and needs updating.

It's not a cliffhanger, although at first I felt it was, but in the true sense, you know where the Trio are, and you know what's going to happen next, sort of. There are many other things that need to happen and they won't necessarily be 'safe' on Iron Fan Mountain, but you have an idea of what is coming.

Therefore by that *very* thin logic, not a traditional cliffhanger.

However, the ending of this book jostled the production schedule somewhat. The next story will COLD FRONT which is the romantasy (yes, yes) which is going to be followed by SAINTS & MONKS (M&S 26), because the gap between these two books should NOT be too long.

After that, I'll jump into STONE and follow that up with MAGES & MONSTERS (M&S 27). At this point we are into next year (2025) which will continue with DIVINE HELL (Night Warden).

Most of this is set, but some of it might be subject to change depending on LIFE, of course. The Patreon story (THE BUREAU) will turn into a full novel next year(CONFLICT RESOLUTION) and I promise to finish off some of the novella trilogies. All of these stories have to revolve around M&S.

I just imagined another, more accurate metaphor for the series of stories I write. Think of M&S as the hypergiant star in the center (think UY Scuti or Stephenson 2-18, for all of us science geeks/nerds out there) and all of the other stories are the planets in orbit in the M&S Universe. Some of those planets are large and some small, but all revolve around M&S.

All of that is to say that there are many stories coming, this and next year (and the years after that). Some I can share now with you, and some are in development, but as long as I can write I will share them all with you.

This next part I repeat often because I find it to be profoundly true. Please forgive me for stating it again and know that I mean it all.
You are totally amazing.

As always, I couldn't do this incredibly insane adventure without you (really I couldn't), my amazing reader. You jump into these adventures with me, when I say "WHAT IF?" you say: "Hmmm what if indeed! LET's GO FIND OUT!

For that, I humbly and deeply thank you.

I consider myself deeply fortunate to have the most

amazing readers that are willing to leap into these worlds with the same reckless abandon I have in writing them.

You truly spoil me.

Few writers I know have such incredible readers that make it possible to explore creating new worlds, introducing different characters, with an incredible group of readers willing to give the new world and characters a chance.

Thank you so much for joining me as we load up the extra thermos (better bring three or six of them—industrial-sized) filled with the delicious inky Death Wish Javambrosia, some of you can call shotgun, but a few of you are going to have to shove the enormous hellhound in the back of the Dark Goat over if you want a seat (bring plenty of sausage/pastrami-for a guaranteed seat!), as we strap in to jump into all sorts of adventures!

There's a long way to go and a short time to get there, we have plans to disrupt, powers to learn, people to rescue, mages to anger, and property to renovate!

Again, I want you to know that this adventure is incredible, but it's made even more incredible by having you on it with me.

I humbly, deeply, and profoundly thank you.

In the immortal sage words of our resident Zen Hellhound Master...

Meat is Life!

gratias tibi ago

Thank you again for jumping into this story with me!

JOIN US

Facebook
Montague & Strong Case Files

Youtube
Bitten Peaches Publishing Storyteller

Instagram
bittenpeaches

Email
orlando@orlandoasanchez.com

M&S World Store
Emandes

SUPPORT US

Patreon
The Magick Squad

Website/Newsletter
www.orlandoasanchez.com

BITTEN PEACHES PUBLISHING

Thanks for Reading!
If you enjoyed this book, would you please **leave a review** at the site you purchased it from? It doesn't have to be long... just a line or two would be fantastic and it would really help me out.

Bitten Peaches Publishing offers more books and audiobooks
across various genres including: urban fantasy, science fiction, adventure, & mystery!

www.BittenPeachesPublishing.com

More books by Orlando A. Sanchez

Montague & Strong Detective Agency Novels
Tombyards & Butterflies•Full Moon Howl•Blood is Thicker•Silver Clouds Dirty Sky•Homecoming•Dragons & Demigods•Bullets & Blades•Hell Hath No Fury•Reaping Wind•The Golem•Dark Glass•Walking the

Razor•Requiem•Divine Intervention•Storm Blood•Revenant•Blood Lessons•Broken Magic•Lost Runes•Archmage•Entropy•Corpse Road•Immortal•Outcast•Shieldbearer

Montague & Strong Detective Agency Stories
No God is Safe•The Date•The War Mage•A Proper Hellhound•The Perfect Cup•Saving Mr. K

Night Warden Novels
Wander•ShadowStrut•Nocturne Melody

Rule of the Council
Blood Ascension•Blood Betrayal•Blood Rule

The Warriors of the Way
The Karashihan•The Spiritual Warriors•The Ascendants•The Fallen Warrior•The Warrior Ascendant•The Master Warrior

John Kane
The Deepest Cut•Blur•Stone

Sepia Blue
The Last Dance•Rise of the Night•Sisters•Nightmare•Nameless•Demon

Chronicles of the Modern Mystics
The Dark Flame•A Dream of Ashes

The Treadwell Supernatural Directive
The Stray Dogs•Shadow Queen•Endgame Tango

Brew & Chew Adventures
Hellhound Blues

Bangers & Mash
Bangers & Mash

Tales of the Gatekeepers
Bullet Ballet•The Way of Bug•Blood Bond

Division 13
The Operative•The Magekiller

Blackjack Chronicles
The Dread Warlock•Deathdancers

The Assassin's Apprentice
The Birth of Death

Gideon Shepherd Thrillers
Sheepdog

DAMNED
Aftermath

Nyxia White
They Bite•They Rend•They Kill

Iker the Cleaner
Iker the Unseen•Daystrider•Nightwalker

Fate of the Darkmages
Fated Fury

Stay up to date with new releases!
Shop www.orlandoasanchez.com for more books and audiobooks!

ART SHREDDERS

I want to take a moment to extend a special thanks to the ART SHREDDERS.

No book is the work of one person. I am fortunate enough to have an amazing team of advance readers and shredders.

Thank you for giving of your time and keen eyes to provide notes, insights, answers to the questions, and corrections (dealing wonderfully with my extreme dreaded comma allergy). You help make every book and story go from good to great. Each and every one of you helped make this book fantastic, and I couldn't do this without each of you.

THANK YOU

<u>ART SHREDDERS</u>

Amber, Audrey Cienki
   Bethany Showell, Beverly Collie
   Cat Inglis, Chris Christman II

Davina Noble, Dawn McQueen Mortimer, Diane Craig, Dolly, Donna Young Hatridge

Hal Bass, Helen

Jasmine Breeden, Jasmine Davis, Jeanette Auer, Jen Cooper, Joy Kiili, Julie Peckett

Karen Hollyhead

Luann Zipp

Malcolm Robertson, Melissa Miller, Michelle Blue

Paige Guido

RC Battels, Rob Farnham, Rohan Gandhy

Sondra Massey, Stacey Stein, Susie Johnson

Tami Cowles, Terri Adkisson

Vikki Brannagan

Wendy Schindler

PATREON SUPPORTERS

Exclusive short stories
Premium Access to works in progress
Free Ebooks for select tiers

Join here
The Magick Squad

THANK YOU

Alisha Harper, Amber Dawn Sessler, Angela Tapping, Anne Morando, Anthony Bock, Anthony Hudson, Ashley Britt

Brenda French, Brett Morse

Carolyn J. Evans, Carrie O'Leary, Christopher Scoggins, Cindy Deporter, Connie Cleary, Cooper Walls

Dan Bergemann, Dan Fong, Daniel Harkavy, David Mitchell,

Davis Johnson, Dawn Bender, Diane Garcia, Di Hara, Diane Jackson, Diane Kassmann, Dorothy Phillips

E.A., Elizabeth Varga, Enid Rodriguez, Eric Maldonado, Eve Bartlet, Ewan Mollison

Federica De Dominicis, Fluff Chick Productions, Fred Westfall

Gail Ketcham Hermann, Gary McVicar, Groove72

Heidi Wolfe

Ingrid Schijven

James Burns, James Wheat, Jasmine Breeden, Jasmine Davis, Jeffrey Juchau, JF, Jim Couger, Jo Dungey, Joe Durham, John Fauver(*in memoriam*), Joy Kiili, Just Jeanette

Kathy Ringo, Krista Fox

Leona Jackson, Lisa Simpson, Lizzette Piltch

Malcolm Robertson, Marie Stein, Mark Morgan, Mark Price, Mary Beth Wright, MaryAnn Sims, Maureen McCallan, Mel Brown, Melissa Miller, Meri, Duncanson

Paige Guido, Patricia Pearson, Patrick Hurley, Peter Griffin, Pete Peters

Rachel Buchanan, Ralph Kroll, Renee Penn, Rick Clapp, Robert Walters

Samantha Rense, Sara M Branson, Sara N Morgan, Sarah Sofianos, Sassy Bear, Sharon Elliott, Shelby, Sherry, Sonyia Roy, Stacey Stein, Steven Huber, Suma, Susan Bowin, Susan Spry

Tami Cowles, Terri Adkisson, Tommy, Trish Brown

Valerie Jondahl, Van Nebedum

W S Dawkins, Wendy Schindler

***

I want to extend a special note of gratitude to all of our Patrons in
The Magick Squad.

Your generous support helps me to continue on this amazing adventure called 'being an author'.

I deeply and truly appreciate each of you for your selfless act of patronage.

You are all amazing beyond belief.

THANK YOU

ACKNOWLEDGEMENTS

With each book, I realize that every time I learn something about this craft, it highlights so many things I still have to learn. Each book, each creative expression, has a large group of people behind it.

This book is no different.

Even though you see one name on the cover, it is with the knowledge that I am standing on the shoulders of the literary giants that informed my youth, and am supported by my generous readers who give of their time to jump into the adventures of my overactive imagination.

I would like to take a moment to express my most sincere thanks:

To Dolly: My wife and greatest support. You make all this possible each and every day. You keep me grounded when I get lost in the forest of ideas. Thank you for asking the right questions when needed, and listening intently when I go off on tangents. Thank you for who you are and the space you create—I love you.

To my Tribe: You are the reason I have stories to tell. You cannot possibly fathom how much and how deeply I love you all.

To Lee: Because you were the first audience I ever had. I love you, sis.

To the Logsdon Family: The words *thank you* are insufficient to describe the gratitude in my heart for each of you. JL, your support always demands I bring my best, my A-game, and produce the best story I can. Both you, Lorelei (my Uber Jeditor), and Audrey, are the reason I am where I am today. My thank you for the notes, challenges, corrections, advice, and laughter. Your patience is truly infinite. *Arigato-gozaimasu.*

To The Montague & Strong Case Files Group—AKA The MoB (Mages of Badassery): When I wrote T&B there were fifty-five members in The MoB. As of this release, there are over one thousand seven-hundred members in the MoB. I am honored to be able to call you my MoB Family. Thank you for being part of this group and M&S.

You make this possible. **THANK YOU.**

To the ever-vigilant PACK: You help make the MoB...the MoB. Keeping it a safe place for us to share and just...be. Thank you for your selfless vigilance. You truly are the Sentries of Sanity.

Chris Christman II: A real-life technomancer who makes the **MoB Kaffeeklatsch** amazing. Thank you for your tireless work and wisdom. Everything is connected...you totally rock!

To the WTA—The Incorrigibles: JL, Ben Z., Eric QK., S.S., and Noah.

They sound like a bunch of badass misfits, because they are. My exposure to the deranged and deviant brain trust you all represent helped me be the author I am today. I have officially gone to the *dark side* thanks to all of you. I humbly give you my thanks, and…it's all your fault.

To my fellow Indie Authors: I want to thank each of you for creating a space where authors can feel listened to, and encouraged to continue on this path. A rising tide lifts all the ships indeed.

To The English Advisory: Aaron, Penny, Carrie, Davina, and all of the UK MoB. For all things English…thank you.

To DEATH WISH COFFEE: This book (and *every* book I write) has been fueled by generous amounts of the only coffee on the planet (and in space) strong enough to power my very twisted imagination. Is there any other coffee that can compare? I think not. DEATH WISH—thank you!

To Deranged Doctor Design: Kim, Darja, Tanja, Jovana, and Milo (Designer Extraordinaire).

If you've seen the covers of my books and been amazed, you can thank the very talented and gifted creative team at DDD. They take the rough ideas I give them, and produce incredible covers that continue to surprise and amaze me. Each time, I find myself striving to write a story worthy of the covers they produce. DDD, you embody professionalism and creativity. Thank you for the great service and spectacular covers. **YOU GUYS RULE!**

To you, the reader: I was always taught to save the best for last. I write these stories for **you**. Thank you for jumping down the rabbit holes of *what if?* with me. You are the reason I write the stories I do.

You keep reading...I'll keep writing.

Thank you for your support and encouragement.

SPECIAL MENTIONS

To Dolly: my rock, anchor, and inspiration. Thank you...always.

Larry & Tammy—The WOUF: Because even when you aren't there...you're there.

Larry & Tammy: Also for **hellitosis,** because what other word could describe hellhound breath...really?

Jeanette: Because no one should travel anywhere without a handy towel. Especially if you're prone to panic lol :).

Orlando A. Sanchez
www.orlandoasanchez.com

Orlando has been writing ever since his teens when he was immersed in creating scenarios for playing Dungeons and Dragons with his friends every weekend.

The worlds of his books are urban settings with a twist of the paranormal lurking just behind the scenes and with generous doses of magic, martial arts, and mayhem.

He currently resides in Queens, NY with his wife and children.

<u>Thanks for Reading!</u>

If you enjoyed this book
Please leave a review & share!
(with everyone you know)

It would really help us out!

Made in the USA
Monee, IL
22 October 2024